# No Use Crying

**For Andy,**

**and for Philip and Bridget**



First published in Great Britain in 2011 and in the USA in 2012 in by
Frances Lincoln Children's Books, 4 Torriano Mews,
Torriano Avenue, London NW5 2RZ
www.franceslincoln.com



A catalogue record for this book is available from the British Library.

ISBN 978-1-84780-214-9

Printed in Croydon, Surrey, UK by CPI Bookmarque Ltd. in July 2011

1 3 5 7 9 8 6 4 2

# No Use Crying

Zannah Kearns

F
FRANCES LINCOLN
CHILDREN'S BOOKS

# ONE

'So, what did Mrs K want?' Akiko asked, rhythmically kicking her school bag as she waited for Niki outside the school gates.

'Oh,' Niki sighed and fell into step as they headed towards the bus stop. 'She just wanted to check that when she said our stories should be *interesting*, I understood that she meant the right sort of interesting.'

'Ah.'

'The wrong sort of interesting gets you seen by psychologists who make you share your feelings with the use of puppets. As if I'd forget *that*.'

'Sounds kinda fun. . . So, no more window cleaners cutting off your mother's head then?'

''Fraid not.'

'Shame.'

'I can't believe she's still *fussing* about it,' Niki said. 'It was in Year *Six* – before I was even in the senior part of the school! Do you think I'm *still* the talk of the staffroom after all this time? The weird freak girl with her free place and psycho personality – wouldn't want me poisoning the minds of all the precious posh kids at perfect St Magda's.'

'Maybe she's scared that in your next story you'll be chopping *her* to pieces.'

'Now there's a thought.'

'And, hey! I'm one of those precious posh kids, thank you very much,' Akiko added, feigning hurt.

'Well, be warned – you don't want to get sucked into *my* imagination. It's darker than a witch's armpit.'

'What a delightful thought. Come on, we're going to miss the bus.'

♠♠♠♠

'Am I in trouble?' Niki had asked when everyone else got their stories back and she didn't. Her first week in a new school – a private all-girls school at that, where she felt totally out of place – and already she was in trouble. 'Please don't tell my mum.'

'It's OK, dear, don't panic,' Mrs Hughes had said, already standing up to address the class. 'But I do need a little chat with your mother, nothing to worry about. Now sit down, it's time for our weather project.'

Niki didn't care about the weather, she just wanted to get her story back and to have never written it.

At the time she had been compelled to write it – it had filled her head, like so many dreams that had haunted her long into the following day. There he'd been, the man on the patio, cleaning the windows. She was watching TV while he stood outside the patio doors, soaping them in great arcs with his big windscreen wiper thing. She'd found herself looking up to watch the soap dribble down the window, sliding in ever-changing shapes. He took hold of another wiper and in a few deft sweeps the window was clear again, mopped and dazzling. So clear, it seemed as if there were no glass at all, only air.

She'd glanced up, and found herself looking straight into his eyes, the eyes of this man with his wipers and rags and buckets, and he'd smiled at her. It felt as though there was nothing between them, no window at all, nothing to stop him stepping into the room and smothering her mouth with that grey rag – shoving it right down her throat so that she couldn't even whimper. Chopping her up and hiding her in his bucket then taking her home and eating her.

Niki had run from the room, along the hall and into the bedroom where she'd propped a chair underneath the door handle. She'd seen someone do that on TV once and was surprised at how it really locked the door. Sitting with her back against the wardrobe so that she could see both the door and the window, she wrote her story. As she wrote, her imagination pulled her into darker images. She pictured him killing her mother first so that there was no one to protect her; cutting off her head, his smile never leaving his face.

She wrote about hiding in an attic, about it being as dark as bats' wings, about hearing his feet on the stairs, about darkness and noises getting closer.

She'd written it because she didn't want it inside her head. It felt as though if she got it all out on paper, every horrible detail, then it would be gone, purged, like when they shoved old junk into plastic sacks for the bin men, hurling them far from the house. It had never occurred to her that it would cause so much trouble.

♦♦♦♦

'So, what's it going to be?' Akiko asked, just before it was time for Niki to get off at her stop. 'Skinning puppies? Boiling bunnies?'

'You're sicker than I am, reject.'

'Just checking, just checking.'

'Just because I'm the daughter of a heinous criminal, doesn't mean I'm a psycho myself, you know.'

Niki didn't know when it had first started – making jokes about her father – but each time she felt a prickling sensation inside her. It simply wasn't funny, however much she pretended not to care.

'That's what they all say,' said Akiko narrowing her eyes in mock suspicion. 'See you on Monday, freak.'

'Yeah, have a good weekend, loser.'

Niki walked from the bus stop up to the Munroes' massive house, where she and her mum were living. All her life, Niki and her mum, Angela, had travelled from house to house, her mum working as a private carer for the elderly. They had rarely stayed anywhere for longer than a couple of school terms – before too long people found out that Niki's dad was an 'unsavoury character' and Angela would move them on. The fact they had no contact with him made no difference. As soon as the whispering began, *murder, drugs, prison* – perhaps Niki's teacher letting slip to a mum at a Pilates class one Saturday morning – Angela would start to look for work elsewhere. 'It's just easier this way,' she'd say to Niki.

This was the longest that Niki had lived in one place. Two years. Professor Munroe was dying slowly of a disease that took away all his physical abilities – he couldn't walk or use his arms, and could hardly speak. His wife, Beatrice, had once been Headmistress of St Magdalena's, and she had made it possible for Niki to be given a free place at the school.

Popper, the Munroes' Jack Russell, tore down the driveway and leapt into Niki's arms, twisting and struggling in an attempt to lick her face.

'All right, calm *down*, Pops! You'd think this wasn't something we went through every single day!' Niki laughed.

She went in through the back door and shrugged off her coat, then scooped Popper up, stroking her cheek against his smooth coat while he shook all over in a frenzy of tail wagging.

'We'll worry about homework in a bit, Pops. I just want to collapse for a while.' She wandered towards the kitchen in search of her mum and a snack.

'It's not like I have a choice!' she heard her mother saying. 'My hands are tied.'

Angie's angry tone caused Niki to pause in the hallway just outside the kitchen's open door.

'Oh, don't talk rot – "your hands are tied". Honestly!' Beatrice Munroe clattered mugs into a sink of soapy water that was so hot it flushed her skin. She fussed the water to get more bubbles, then turned to look at Angela.

'You could always leave Niki here, you know. *You* go. She could visit in the holidays, and you could come here whenever you needed a break.'

'I couldn't do that!' said Angela. 'It wouldn't be good for her. And I love her too much.'

'You think this is love, do you – taking away the best opportunity she's ever had? She's on a *full* scholarship at one of the best private schools around! She's thriving, Angela. You can see how much she's settled. She's spent her whole life moving from place to place – you yourself have been worrying about her never having had a proper home. What will it do to her to be uprooted yet again?

'And anyway, how long has he got? I don't mean to be macabre, but if it's only a matter of weeks or months then it seems ridiculous to take Niki away when maybe you won't even have to be gone that long.'

Angie gripped her mug of now cold coffee and pressed her lips together.

'Children go to boarding school all the time,' continued Beatrice. 'She could visit you some – probably *most* – weekends. The trains are very good.'

'She needs her mother.'

'She'll still *have* her mother! Terms are short – she'd be with you at half-term and for all the long holidays. She can stay here in term times, so it wouldn't even be like proper boarding. She *loves* it here.'

'Now who's speaking out of mixed motives?'

Niki hugged Popper tighter. Through the crack on the hinge side of the door, she could make out a line of Beatrice's body as she stood by the kitchen window.

'I'm sorry, Bea,' said Angie after a moment, 'but my mind's made up.'

'You honestly think this is the best thing for her? Taking her back to the root of all your upsets? That's good mothering, is it?'

'Hey, I've always done my best for my daughter. I might not have a degree or a *wing* of a *school* named after me—'

'Oh, come on, Angela, I'm not putting you down. Don't make this about something it isn't. You're the best home help we've ever had, and that's not patronising, that's not degrading. Degrading is having your arse wiped by a stranger, and not being able to bloody well swallow without spitting food all down your front.'

'Bea.'

'I just thought you'd be with us until the end,' Beatrice said quietly. 'Peter loves you. You've been so *good* for him – for both of us. You've looked after him so well. The thought of another nurse. . .'

'You'll need another nurse soon, anyway, a proper one. I won't be able to look after him when things get . . . well, you know.'

'But I thought you might stay on anyway, that you'd be here till Niki finished secondary school, did her A-levels, got into university. You could find another job and lodge with us – go in for nursing or whatever you wanted, you're still young. That way Niki can stay where she's happy. It's not good to move her again.'

Niki heard the scrape of her mum's chair as she stood up. Along the hall she could see the outside light shining fuzzily through the small square of frosted glass in the front door. It was October and already getting dark noticeably earlier.

Out of the corner of her eye she sensed something move and turned to see Professor Munroe roll his electric wheelchair out of his study. They looked at each other and kept silent, listening together.

Niki couldn't understand why her mother was so adamant they had to move again, it didn't make sense. Why *must* they go? *Why* was there no choice? It wasn't like Mrs M wanted to get rid of them.

Well, I won't go, Niki thought; it was as simple as that.

'Why couldn't he come here – there'd be room for him?'

'You don't know my dad, Bea. He'd never agree to it.'

Niki looked straight up at Peter and could tell from his eyes, despite his deadpan face, that he was as surprised as she was. Her mum's *dad*? Her mum didn't have a dad – he'd died before Niki was born. Both her grandparents had. Her mum didn't like talking about it, but they had definitely died way back, that much she knew.

'When I saw Mum four years ago. . .'

Niki felt sick.

'. . . she made me promise to take care of him. It was her dying wish. Despite everything, I promised that I would do the right thing by him, for Mum's sake. And so this is it. My mind's made up.'

'So when are you going to tell her?' Beatrice said, sounding old and tired, and as though the house were already emptier.

'I don't know,' Angie said. 'How am I going to explain about Dad? Maybe I should just say he's someone else we're going to care for.'

At this Niki bent forward and let Popper jump onto the floor, his claws scraping on the slate flagstones as he scrabbled into the kitchen. Angie and Bea looked up, startled to find Niki standing in the doorway.

'What, so you're going to tell me another lie?' she said to her mum.

Angie began, 'Niki, love—'

'Don't bother,' Niki said, 'I wouldn't believe you anyway.'

'Why don't you both go and feed the horses?' Beatrice asked, holding up the key to the feed shed.

Niki glared at them, then ran upstairs, slamming her bedroom door as hard as she could before opening it and slamming it a second time.

Being lied to by her own mum! It wasn't something Niki had ever imagined possible. She'd never lied about anything important to her mum.

It had always been the two of them together. But this wasn't even just some little fib. This was lying about having parents alive. Her mother had deceived her for Niki's entire life!

Sitting down on her bed, Niki tried to count them – how many untrue things had her mother said? Not just direct lies, but those implied false promises – like the one about their not moving again, about her not having to change schools again if she didn't want to.

But it was the lie about her grandparents that troubled Niki the most. It seemed so strange – keeping her grandparents secret. What had she meant 'despite everything'? And now they were going to go and live with this man who was meant to be her grandad.

What would Professor and Mrs Munroe do without them? The place had become home, Mrs M was right. Niki was the best at understanding the professor's slurred speech – Beatrice often made mistakes or had to bend over him for an embarrassingly long time saying, 'What was that, darling? Say that just once more.' And then Professor Munroe would sit back in frustration and shake his head while Niki was called in from the garden. Were they really going to abandon *them* as well?

There was a knock on the door.

'Can I come in?'

Niki hugged her knees tighter and bit her lip, staring in front of her as though she could burn a hole in the wall.

'Niki.' Angie came to the bed, but stopped short of sitting down, shifting instead from foot to foot.

'So . . . dead before I was born?' Niki said, after the silence had become awkward.

'He's made quite the recovery,' Angie said, giving a weak laugh. 'Sorry. I don't know what to say. We had a very difficult relationship – he'd never have seen us, and it just seemed easier, less painful, to make believe that he didn't exist. Does that make sense?'

'No.'

'Oh, love – the thing is—'

'So where's Grandma?'

'Well, she did die. . . But, actually, you met her a few times.'

'How do you mean?'

'Do you remember Granny Smith?'

Every year, sometimes a couple of times, they had met up with Granny Smith. Angela told Niki she had cared for her through a broken hip when Niki was just a baby. Smith was a common enough name, so Niki had never suspected they might be related. They had kept in touch, meeting for tea in a café or a walk around a zoo. Granny Smith had always sent Niki Christmas and birthday presents, often expensive things. Niki had wondered why her mum let Granny Smith keep doing it when she didn't let the other people they had cared for buy her gifts.

Niki had loved Granny Smith, written to her, tapped her photo for luck right up to the time when Angie had told her she had died.

She didn't know what she would have done differently if she'd known Granny Smith was her real grandma, but it still mattered. It mattered that she had known this lady for so long – and yet had never known her.

'So, if you hate your dad why are we going to look after him?'

'I don't *hate* him exactly. We just fell out. I promised Mum I'd look after him if he ever needed it. She loved him and, well, he's family.'

'Where does he live?'

'London. But, listen, Niki, Beatrice is right. You have such great opportunities here. All I've done is make you move from place to place to place. You'll never go to a better school than St Magda's. I can't rob you of all that you have here.

'We can work out your coming to London in the holidays. And, I mean, if . . . well, if Dad hasn't got long then I might be back pretty soon, anyway.'

London. Even the word sounded big.

Niki looked up at her mum, small and pale – so different from how she looked herself. The woman who'd given birth to her at just sixteen – dropping out of school, raising her baby alone. It was obvious why Angie had fallen out with her dad – why else would she have lied to Niki about her grandparents? And now her mum was expected to go and face – go and *care* for – this father who'd rejected his own daughter, all because of her.

'So, when are we going?'

'Niki, I just said—'

'I know.'

'But what if you hate it?'

'I'll sulk. And guilt-trip you into buying me an iPod.'

'In your dreams.' Angela fell onto the bed and pulled Niki into a hug. 'Thank you. I don't know how I'd have done it without you.'

'So, when *are* we going?'

'I guess half-term makes sense. . . That's just two weeks away – I need to start phoning round schools.

There's so much to do. Oh, love, I'm so *relieved* you're coming. You and me, hey? Nothing's going to drive us apart.' Angie smiled and kissed the top of Niki's head.

Niki leant into her mum's hug, still clutching her knees, staring off somewhere into the carpet. Just when she thought they had finally found a home, everything was going to change all over again.

# TWO

The escalator glided Niki and her mother up to the tube exit. Niki was in front, squashed behind a woman with skittle shaped legs – crackably skinny ankles up into bulbous thighs that looked as hard as wood in her white skin-tight jeans. Black lady. Her bottom was like a bowling ball – as high and round as could be. Niki's mum hardly had a bum – in jeans her back seemed to go straight down into her legs. Niki, on the other hand, had a Caribbean behind. 'A backside like Beyoncé's,' Akiko had once teased her.

People pushed to get through the ticket barriers as quickly as possible, sighing theatrically at Niki and her mum's slowness to find their tickets. A gangly teenager squeezed through with the person in front, avoiding having to pay. Niki and her mum were pushed forward by the surge of bodies, out into a mish-mash of flower sellers, newspaper stands, passers-by – all milling round a statue of

Niki-had-no-idea-who that stood right in everyone's way. The roads were crammed with buses, bikes and cars overstuffed with passengers. Pedestrians stepped into the roads, forcing cars to break sharply.

Marks and Spencer, The Co-op and Greggs bakery neon signs fuzzed round the edges in the drizzle. Far more noticeable to Niki were all the unfamiliar shops – one-off businesses which had messily hand-painted boards stuck above doorways. Their windows were filled with scribbled notices about the special offers inside, hand-scrawled posters pasted wonkily alongside stickers about lottery tickets and Oyster travel cards. Niki peered through a doorway – shelves of biscuits, giant sacks of rice, barrels of cooking oil, everything in unfamiliar packaging.

Fast food booths gushed out greasy air. Everywhere she looked she felt as though she were transported somewhere new – Africans, Indians, Asians, white people who didn't look English, Jamaicans, Londoners with gold teeth and a cigarette pallor to their skin.

There seemed to be an endless succession of Asian and Caribbean convenience stores with crates of plantain, yams, papayas and avocados stacked on fake grass matting with prices marked on bits of ripped up cardboard box.

From the Indian shops, joss sticks snaked wisps of smoke through their open doorways, cloying Niki's throat. Curry house after curry house – Radha Krishna, Sree Krishna, Lahore Karahi, she tried sounding the words. Through their tinted windows Niki could see shrines to multi-armed gods, garlands of paper flowers adorning their necks, a painting of a woman with a baby suckling her breast, her free hand held up with her fingers poised in a very particular way.

They passed a giant bingo hall – its sign garish blue and yellow that didn't fit with the style of the building.

'Used to be a cinema in Dad's day,' said Angie. 'In fact, the Rolling Stones played there, if you can believe it.'

'It's hard to believe anything you say,' Niki muttered so that Angie couldn't hear.

Over the road she saw an enormous halal butcher's – its shutters pulled up leaving only a corner column, so that the whole place was exposed to the street, showing its counters filled with lines and lines of goose-pimpled chicken flesh.

And the people! As she adjusted to all she was

seeing, Niki began to distinguish faces. Since living at the Munroes' in their little hamlet of Oakley, Niki's only experience of 'city' had been occasional trips to Bath. She realised how used she'd grown to being surrounded by white people. By a certain type of white person. Neat adults who wore well-pressed clothes, all sharp angles and expensive accessories. And the predominantly white girls at her school – girls with over-brushed hair who liked wearing baggy jumpers and loose scarves draped around their necks.

At her school she had been the only person with any sort of Caribbean ethnicity. There had been quite a lot of Kenyans, a few Chinese, Japanese, even a pair of Russian twins, a couple of mixed-race English-Malay students, a Korean, Europeans and some English girls who'd grown up in Paraguay. But Afro-Caribbeans had been the noticeable exception.

She had never seen so many black and mixed-race people before now. It was strange to walk along and realise that she probably blended in more than her mother.

In Bath and around Oakley, most people had fitted a certain nondescript type – so normal, so expected – there had been few surprises to anyone's appearance.

Rarely had a face shocked her. Here Niki felt like she was walking through a cast of make-believe characters – as if she were seeing people through the warped reflections of fairground mirrors. Crumpled faces, squished like plasticine, sagging, swollen bodies. Teenage mums pushing their babies, surrounded by mates. Girls with their hair scraped back so the ridges of combs could still be seen in it, crisp with hairspray, ears full of hoops and cheap jewellery, muffin tops of flesh spilling out over low cut jeans. Many were wearing cropped bomber jackets with hood trims that must once have looked like fake fur and now resembled matted mongrel hair. Large women with gigantic bosoms wearing just T-shirts – *no bras!* – their mammoth boobs lolloping about, pulling down their entire torsos – falling to their *waists* almost – their nipples scooting off at crazy angles like pairs of goggly eyes.

Niki's shoulder ached from dragging her suitcase on its little wheels. It kept tipping over on the lips of uneven paving stones, twisting her arm. The drizzle was beginning to turn to rain and the dampness she could feel soaking through her jeans seemed to precisely reflect her feeling of misery.

'This way,' said Angie, turning off the high street and along a road of terraced houses.

Angie stopped suddenly and Niki heard her take a deep breath – it was raggedy, the nerves showing through. In the last fortnight of getting ready for this move, it hadn't really occurred to Niki to think how her mum might be feeling about seeing her dad again. All she'd thought about was leaving behind her friends, the Munroes, Popper. About how *she* felt going to live with this man who had never wanted to know her.

She was surprised to think of her mum as being nervous – to think of her mum's history, her life before anything Niki had known.

She looked at her and asked, 'Are you ready for this?'

Angie gave an unconvincing smile. 'Well, it's now or never, hey, love?' She laughed, then almost immediately fell silent, her face losing any hint of a smile. 'The last time I was here was for your grandma's funeral four years ago – and then I only stayed for about half an hour after the service, sat in the front room and then left. I barely spoke a word to him.'

They were standing at a crossroad. Niki wasn't sure exactly which house her mum was looking at. Then she saw the curtains move in a house on the road opposite.

It was fenced in by wrought iron railings. Shallow steps led up to a porch, the bottom half of which was white plastic, the top half double-glazed windows. It looked to Niki like a greenhouse stuck randomly onto the front. Inside this porch were spider plants and cacti resting along the windowsills, and a high-backed armchair. The wooden door inside the porch had no window and was varnished a dark, ugly brown. It looked like a door that didn't get opened very often.

They walked across side by side, the only sound the trundling of suitcase wheels. Angie rang the doorbell and then they both stood back, one step below the top, bags in hand.

It took him several tugs to pull open the front door, confirming to Niki that he didn't go out much. Angie's mouth was open, obviously with a greeting prepared on her lips, but it seemed to stick in her throat, and they all stood staring at each other through the glass of the porch door.

'Well, you don't look as though you're dying,' Angie said at last.

'Are you coming in, then?'

Her grandad didn't look at Niki. His eyes stayed

fixed on Angie as they walked through the door, and then at his shoes as he stepped back to let them past. Setting their bags in the hallway next to the stairs, Niki followed her mother into the sitting room.

'Good journey?'

'Fine, thanks. I wouldn't say no to a cup of tea.' Angie walked through some open double-doors at the back of the sitting room into the kitchen. Niki followed, hearing the slippered shuffle of her grandad close behind.

She was struck by how alike he and her mother looked – both slight-framed and short. He had no hair on top, just feeble wisps round the edges, and in fact Angie's blonde hair was thin and fell in lank strands so that you could see light through it. They were both starkly pale. Niki's skin had never felt so dark, her height so stretched, her hair so frizzy. She knocked over a vase of plastic flowers on the kitchen table and as she reached out to right it again her sleeve pushed over the peppermill.

While he made the tea with clinical precision over on the counter to one side, Niki was able to sit at the table and stare at him. He was speckled with old man's stubble, and beneath she could see his skin itself was an unhealthy, polluted colour with ruby thread-veins lacing his cheeks. His lips were a slippery pink and he kept rolling them together, moistening them with his tongue as he spooned loose tea into a brown enamel teapot. The rims of his eyes were red and it looked as though he didn't have any eyelashes.

He struggled to open a tin of biscuits. It became embarrassing and Angie reached out to take it from him, saying, 'Come here,' but then with a triumphant *ffffut* the tin opened and he banged it down onto the table before shuffling to the fridge to get out one lonely pint of milk. Niki found herself eating a stale custard cream. She didn't even like custard creams. Inside his fridge, she had seen that there was nothing save that single pint of milk, a withered lettuce and a loaf of bread. She wondered why he kept his bread in the fridge.

The only sounds were the hum of the boiler and the ticking of a clock.

'So, what have you got then? Cancer?'

Niki was shocked to hear her mum speak to an old person like this.

Her grandad raised his eyebrows, pursing his lips into a sort of smile – a defenceless, attacked expression.

'How long have they given you?'

'It's hard to say,' he said, pressing his lips together again. His raised eyebrows caused deep furrows across his forehead, right up into his bald scalp.

Angie picked up her teacup and rested it against the edge of her mouth, casting her gaze out of the window at the soggy lawn and a sky so pale it was as though it were missing.

Niki nibbled the edge of her biscuit, trying to avoid the sickly cream that sandwiched the two sides together. She put it down on the saucer of her cup and then picked it up again, needing something to occupy her fingers. The clock's ticks filled the room, highlighting their silence.

She wished Popper would rush yapping through the door, jump onto her lap and demand that she play with him.

♠♠♠♠

When they'd left The Grange, Mrs M had been holding Popper in her arms. She walked over to Niki and held him out to her.

'You take him. He's your dog, really.'

Niki had looked at them both, chewing her top lip to keep herself from crying. She kissed Popper and he tried to lick her face, jerking his head so that he banged her nose.

'He's happier here,' she said, 'with places to run around.'

She didn't say, 'You're going to need him more than I will,' but over Mrs M's shoulder she could see Professor Munroe slouched in his wheelchair, looking like he might not even see Christmas.

'I'll come and visit him soon.'

'You make sure you do. Popper would fall apart if he thought he'd never see you again.' Mrs M shifted Popper to beneath one arm and pulled Niki into her pillow-soft bosom, squeezing her as tight as she could. Niki could feel her trembling, smell the scent of talcum powder, and feel the knobbles of her broach pressing into her cheek.

'Mind you keep trying at school, my girl. Don't let your time at Magda's have been a waste, do you hear?'

Niki nodded into her shoulder.

'And you can visit anytime. I can easily send you money for train fares so don't ever think there's an excuse for not visiting. Do you hear me? Now off you go. Quickly.'

'Did you remember to take a photo?' Her mum had asked when they were on the train.

Niki had shaken her head, keeping her gaze fixed out of the window.

♠♠♠♠

They walked up the narrow stairs to see their bedrooms. Niki's grandad now slept in a front room downstairs, across the hallway from the sitting room. Niki had looked in and seen that he had one of those mechanical beds with a mattress that could be set to different angles, making it easier to get in and out.

'That was for when Mum was ill,' Angie said in a low voice.

He took the stairs with painful slowness, gripping the banister as if hauling himself up in the face of a gale.

Niki's room was full of clutter. The wardrobe was stuffed with tweed skirts and woollen cardigans in plastic covers. There were cardboard boxes, shoeboxes, and tied up plastic bags on top of the wardrobe, under the bed and stacked in the corner of the room. The chest of drawers was brimful with blouses and petticoats.

'Where's she meant to put her stuff?' Angie said.

'Yes, I meant to clear it out. We can do that,' said

her grandad over his shoulder, already inching along to the room where Angie would sleep.

'I thought you'd want your old room.'

Angie didn't reply.

Inside was the room of a girl. A bedspread patterned with pink flowers matched the curtains and the colour of the carpet. The walls were covered with posters of pop groups that Niki didn't recognise. China ornaments lined a white shelf above a chest of drawers covered with dusty bottles of moisturiser, a hair brush, a photo of Angie in a leotard holding a certificate and a medal, her parents crouched on either side of her, each with a hand on her shoulder as they all smiled at the camera.

'Why did you keep it like this?' Angie said, her voice shaky, gentle for the first time since she'd arrived.

'I just did. Jeanette does a good job of keeping it clean every now and then, but I usually get her doing other things. It needs a bit of a going over. Still, I suppose you can do that now. I told her I wouldn't be needing her any more.'

And he was gone, leaving Angie in the middle of her room looking around her, slowly picking up objects like a small, lacquered pot, which she held as if it were a newly hatched bird.

Niki stood aside from the doorway to let her grandfather pass. She watched him wander along the corridor. He turned to walk down the stairs so that they were facing each other across open space – the stairs leading down in front of him, she at the other end of the landing. He looked up and paused, one foot already on the step below. He seemed to be waiting for something, but she didn't know what.

'Shall I call you Grandad?' she said.

'If you want.' And, in his brown slippers, he started his slow descent.

# THREE

'You do realise they're going to crucify me at school?' Niki said, on their way home from Ikea. They'd gone to get stuff to transform Niki's room from granny storage unit to teenage girl's personal space, and Niki had been able to maximise on Angie's feelings of guilt to get some pretty cool stuff.

'What makes you say that?' Angie asked in surprise.

'Look at me! *Country Bumpkin* might as well be woven out of my frizz and hung all over with fairy lights.'

'Oh, Niki!' Angie laughed.

'I look like such a reject compared to everyone round here.'

'It's not about how you look, Niki.'

'Mother, please. Don't be naive.'

'Naive! Aren't I meant to be the all-knowing one in these conversations?'

'Like that was ever the case.'

'Er, excuse me!'

'Well, I refuse to go to school until you let me do something about my hair. And buy me some new clothes.'

'You'll be wearing school uniform!'

'New shoes, then. That's what they'll see. That's what they'll *judge* me on. . . My entire school career will be made or broken by what shoes I wear on my first day.'

From Angie's own experience of school, she knew that girls at this age could be complete cows. However pleasant and 'nurturing' St Magda's had been, the reality was that it was hardly the preparation a girl like Niki needed. Like it or not, life was going to be about getting through the day without some older girl stealing your lunch money and smacking your head against a locker. Not extra-curricular oboe.

'Oh, all right,' Angie said. 'You've won me over with your compelling powers of persuasion.'

'Yes, well, my razor-sharp reasoning added to these puppy-dog eyes made it kind of inevitable.'

'Hmm. Twisting and little fingers comes to mind.'

'Who? Me?' Niki grinned and pulled Angie into a hug. 'Thanks, Mama. Honestly, you're saving me from certain death. You should feel proud.'

♠♠♠♠

'So, what's your name, den?'

'Nikita.'

'Ooooh, ain't you summink special!'

'Leave off, Chantelle,' said Janaia.

Janaia was the class representative from 10P sent to collect Niki from the headmaster's office the first day after half-term. Niki's mum had almost kissed her goodbye, had moved towards her, then hesitated when faced with Niki's horrified expression.

Janaia had talked non-stop all the way back to their form room – about how easy it was to get lost, about how there were certain places you just *did not go*, that she'd be safest keeping her head down and sticking with Janaia 'and my girls'. They were all in sets for most subjects so Janaia couldn't be sure who Niki's teachers would be.

Niki didn't say that she'd already been put in the top set for every subject based on her report from St Magdalena's. She just nodded to everything Janaia said and tried to remember the route they were taking so that she'd be able to find her way back in case she wanted to leg it out of there. She wanted to already – run as fast as she could, as far away as possible.

The place looked grim. Gloomy, beige corridors were lit by watery light leaking in through opaque sky-lights. Its sprawling layout was so confusing that soon Niki had no idea which way they'd come. They went up a flight of stairs to a landing where a huge window looked out over some battered netball courts.

'This is our room,' Janaia had said, looking at Niki over her shoulder as she pushed a door open.

Niki had held her breath as she followed Janaia inside.

'So, *Neeky,*' Chantelle said, ignoring Janaia, 'why d'ya talk so posh, den?'

'I just come from a place where they talk like that.' She tried to make her voice more casual, dropping her consonants without being too obvious. Those crisp-ended sounds Mrs M had worked so hard on were now hastily discarded, like her mother's kiss, aborted midair.

'You is a proper neek.' Chantelle walked off, a strawberry lace dangling from her lips like a forgotten strand of spaghetti.

Niki looked after her, envying her sleek hair, tied up with a slender red ribbon. Niki's new cornrows were so tight they were giving her a headache. She liked how they made her look, though – sharper, definitely more street. But they hurt like hell.

'That's the price you pay for beauty,' her mother had teased.

The price for fitting in, Niki had thought, and was now adding to herself, just as long as I keep my mouth shut. All along at St Magda's she'd felt like the common one – the one who couldn't afford riding lessons or to go skiing for Christmas.

And now *I'm* being called posh, I just can't win!

'Don't take any notice of 'er,' Janaia said. 'Chantelle always feels like she gotta say *sumfink*, you know?'

*Sum-fink*. Niki recorded these pronunciations as if she were back learning Latin.

Mr Reese entered and Janaia took Niki over to meet him.

'This is Nikita. Everyone make her welcome,' he shouted in a bored voice.

*'Hiiiii, Nikeeee'aaa.'* The class drew out her name as long and loud as they could and then started giggling. One of the boys wolf-whistled.

'That'll do,' said Mr Reese and waved Niki back to her seat.

♠♠♠♠

'How did it go?' Robert asked when Angie got back from school.

'As bad as I'd imagined,' Angela said, taking the mug of coffee that he held out to her. 'The girl sent to collect Niki looked like she wanted to be a gangsta rapper or something – she'd plucked her eyebrows to nothing, and then pencilled them back in! And she had some sort of shiny *grease* plastering her hair to her head. If Niki comes home saying she wants to look like that I'll die.'

Robert gave a sympathetic smile and busied himself with washing up the breakfast things. He tried to make himself as inconspicuous as possible, hoping that Angie would forget he was there and so stay.

'She was so *fat*, too,' Angie said, almost to herself. 'Janet . . . her name can't have been Janet. Janetta or something. It was like puppy fat to the extreme – she actually had a beer belly. It can't be healthy. I don't ever remember girls being that fat when I was younger.'

'Well, you hung around with the sporty ones,' Robert said. 'All your gym crowd.'

She'd certainly had a gymnast's body – her suppleness getting her nicknamed Elastic Legs and Bendy.

That's as original as they'd got in those days, Angie thought to herself. 'Oi, Bendy.' You always knew a boy liked you if he shouted at you like that.

In her day they'd lived on Diet Coke and apples. It had been easy to skip breakfast and lunch, but for the most part she'd not been able to get out of supper. They'd eaten as a family up until her mid-teens. At six o'clock they'd sit down for tea together and then her mum would head out and do nights – she always worked nights and then every week or so had a string of days off.

When Angie had turned about fourteen she'd managed to start avoiding family meals. She'd get home deliberately late to find her mum had left her food served up and covered with another plate on the sideboard. One time, her dad had come into the kitchen while she was sliding the whole plate-load of food into the bin, tilting it just enough for gravity to take hold, then suddenly realising that he was there watching her. But it was too late, and they looked on together as it all slopped like a depth charge into the freshly-emptied bin, leaving a smear of orange grease across the plate.

'I don't feel well,' she'd said.

'You'd better go to bed.'

Why hadn't he stopped her as she turned sideways to slide past him in the doorway? Not even scolded her for the waste of food. Why hadn't he reached out a hand, drawn her into him and asked what was really going on? Nothing she did seemed to get any sort of response. Stuffing that head of his into the sand – his ostrichy, beaky face. He'd let her slip on by like a cold draught. She had gone upstairs – taking each step as slowly as he did now – and climbed straight into bed with her clothes on and without cleaning her teeth.

When she got pregnant, Angie started eating properly again. Her mum, Betsy, had taken her to the doctor and they'd both emphasised the importance of being healthy for the baby. Almost with the first bite of a sandwich it had felt like her sanity returned and she realised how dangerously close she'd been to developing full-blown anorexia or something. It was frightening to think how much she'd been messing with her body.

When she started to join in family meals again her dad had smiled and nodded to see her eating. To see her body getting a little bit fuller. As if he had been right all along, it had just been a phase.

Soon you'll have something to deal with that you won't be able to avoid, Angie had thought, staring at him while he chewed his dinner. He had avoided dealing with her shrinking body, but what now – when he realised the true reason for her growth?

Niki seemed to love food in a way that Angie had never experienced herself. She couldn't really get so excited about Neapolitan ice cream or rice pudding – sucking it off the spoon the way Niki did, little by little. She knew better than to comment on it, never wanting her to get screwed up over food – to create a problem that currently didn't exist. She had a youthful chubbiness which Angie had to admit suited her. She could see heart-stopping curves forming and those beautiful, rangy legs, those long arms and large palms that she hadn't grown into yet. And her lips. Huge! They looked like lips men would want to squeeze between theirs.

And she was only fourteen! To be thinking these things, seeing these things in her daughter. It was terrifying. She saw men eyeing her up in the street. Niki walked past, oblivious to the impact of her height and sleek face that seemed all sweeping lines, perfect rounds and delicate points.

'How on earth is she getting on?' Angie said suddenly. 'I can't believe she got me to agree to her walking home on her own.'

'She'll be fine.'

'All I can picture is her coming through the door with her tie yanked into a peanut knot, tear-stained face, saying someone's nicked her mobile phone.'

Once when Angie was still at school, a girl had actually had her hair cut off. An enormous fat plait – like a long tenderloin, heavy and gleaming down her back. Hacked with scissors right at the nape of her neck. A boy was expelled.

'How am I going to manage until 3.30?' she wailed, scraping her hands through her hair.

'She'll be *fine,*' Robert repeated.

'Oh, like you even care,' Angie snapped, too anxious for Niki, and angry about all she'd just been remembering to accept any sympathy from him. She pushed back her chair and went up to her room.

What on earth was I thinking, bringing Niki here? Angie asked herself, pacing up and down. She took the small radio from her room and went into the bathroom which she began to clean frantically, turning the volume up high, trying to block out her anxiety.

♦♦♦♦

'Chantelle James, what are you doing at the back?'

'Oh, sorry, Miss, I forgot.'

'I am getting fed *up* with having to say the same thing every week. Come here.'

Chantelle sashayed to the front, swinging her hips as though trying to collide with every desk she walked past.

Niki was in the front row at the only set of desks that had been vacant by the time she found the classroom. Her first lesson of top set Maths. From where she sat she could hear everything Mrs Hennessey was saying.

'What did we agree?'

'Dat I sit at de front and be sweet as a lamb,' Chantelle replied in a theatrical whisper. 'Sorry, Miss, I forgot, innit.'

'If you step out of line just once more – Chantelle, are you listening? Just once more, and you will be out of my class. Do you understand?'

'Yes, Miss, sorry, Miss.'

'Sit next to the new girl. And do *not* push me.'

Niki watched Chantelle saunter over and fall into the chair next to her.

'Hi, Neeky. Long time no see. You in all the top sets, ain't ya, Miss Brainy?'

Niki smiled tightly and carried on doodling

on her Maths book. She was surprised to see someone like Chantelle in top set Maths.

'I ain't so fick, neeva,' Chantelle added, as if reading her mind. 'So, don't go copyin'.' And she pretended to shield her work with her arm.

Niki was drawing Manga cartoons of high-kicking girls with pigtails and eyes the size of saucers, the way Akiko had taught her at St Magda's. She and Akiko had made up all sorts of stories about them. Her mind drifted away from what Mrs Hennessey was trying to teach – she knew equations, anyway, and could finish the exercises without having to hear the explanation.

'Wow, dat's well good,' Chantelle said, leaning over her shoulder. She pushed her school diary towards Niki. 'Do me one.'

Niki drew her a girl with a big Afro and a pet hovering beside her.

'What's dat?'

'A flying possum.'

'Sweet,' grinned Chantelle. 'Man, your books are covered! Dere was me finkin' you were workin' away, but actually you just drawin' pictures. Ha! Maybe you ain't so neek as ya sound, huh?' She gave a sly grin – a *we shall see* sort of smile.

'Well, I guess there's a degree of neekiness that's kind of hard to disguise,' Niki replied. 'But, you know, I'm trying to shake it off.'

'Dat is gonna be one tough job, man. Like I said, you talk so posh!'

'Yeah, well, I *told* you. They were posh where I lived. It's just the way I learnt. You'd talk posh if you'd come from there.'

Chantelle snorted at the idea.

'We lived with rich people,' Niki said. 'My mum was a nurse for them.'

'*My* mum's a nurse! With psychiatric people, though – nutters! My dad's one – a nutter, not a nurse. Well, not like *crazy*-crazy, but he has "Issues". He's in Springfield – d'you know it?'

Niki shook her head. 'D'you ever see him?' she asked, surprised that Chantelle was so happy to admit all of this.

'Yeah, he comes out some weekends or we go out wiv 'im up to the Common or summink. He's all right, just, like, can't cope wiv life, you know? He's not in dere all de time, it varies. But he don't ever live wiv us. He and me mum – well dey're kind of together, I s'pose, but she says 'e could never 'ack our place – ha! Four kids and me mum in dis tiny little house is too much, so 'e has 'is own little flat and we go round dere sometimes for takeaway and stuff. We're what you call "unconventional", innit?' Chantelle laughed and was asked by Mrs Hennessey why this particular equation was causing so much amusement.

'Sorry, Miss.'

'So, your mum is allowed to be a nurse for your *dad*?' Niki asked after they were no longer under Mrs Hennessey's scrutiny.

'Nah. She's on the old people's ward. Dementia and dat. Dey're quite sweet, really. I like old people.'

'Me too!'

'*Girls!* Am I going to have to separate you?'

'No, Miss. Sorry, Miss.'

They began to get on with their calculations, working down the list of exercises. It was easy and they both kept pace. It was fun for Niki to glance over and see Chantelle on the same exercise.

Chantelle looked up and grinned when she got ahead. 'Keep up, neeky girl, if you're so clever.'

They finished but could see that some pupils still had a few exercises to complete.

'So what about *your* dad, den?' Chantelle said after a while.

'Huh?' Niki pretended not to understand.

'My dad's a loon, what about yours? 'Ave you got one?'

Niki bit her lip, drew round the lines of one of her cartoons.

'It's funny you should ask,' she said, after a while.

'*Not* a loon as well?' Chantelle said in disbelief.

'No. . .' Niki took a deep breath.

Here goes nothing, she thought, wondering how long it would be before the whole school knew.

'He's in prison.' She hoped that if Chantelle could admit her dad had mental problems she might understand in some way.

It's not like *I* did anything wrong, Niki thought. She bent lower over her drawing, scrubbing at the paper with her pen. She felt a silky strand of loathing pulling inside her – this man she didn't even know who made her ashamed and afraid.

'What did 'e do?' Chantelle asked after a moment. There was no shock in her voice. She sounded as normal as if Niki had said her dad worked for the post office.

'I don't know exactly,' Niki replied. 'Murder, drugs. My mum *hates* talking about it. But it must have been something bad because he's been in there for over ten years.'

'Shit, man, dat's a long time.'

'*Chantelle!*'

'Oops, Miss. Sorry, Miss.'

Niki went back to drawing cartoons.

''Ere, let me,' Chantelle said, taking Niki's exercise book from her. She drew a cartoon of Mrs Hennessey – big nose, boxy jacket with buttons straining at the front, eyes too close together.

Niki started giggling. She reached over and drew a few stray hairs on the chin.

'Yeah! An' a tash!' said Chantelle, forgetting yet again to keep her voice down.

'Chantelle James!'

'Oops, sorry, Miss. Really.'

'Come *here*!'

'Oh, crap. I is now in serious trouble.' Scraping her chair back noisily, she stood up as though it cost her great effort.

'Bring that book.'

'Aah, Miss. It weren't nuffink.'

'Now!'

Mrs Hennessey looked at the cartoon for quite a while before slowly setting the book down on her desk and raising her eyes to meet Chantelle's.

'I didn't mean it, Miss.'

'You have had warning after warning.'

'But Miss! I hardly done anyfin' dis time!'

'You have – *once again* – shown complete disrespect—'

'But I finished all me work! Dis, honestly, ain't nuffink!'

'You leave me no choice.'

Niki stood up. 'Mrs Hennessey.'

'Not now!'

'I drew it.'

There was silence as the class started to take notice of what was happening. Niki walked up to where Mrs Hennessey was standing.

'I drew the picture,' Niki repeated. 'I'm sorry, it was just a bit of fun.'

'What's your name?'

'Nikita Smith.'

'Well, Miss Smith,' Mrs Hennessey said, casting her eyes down to look at the picture again. 'You need to think long and hard about the sort of reputation you want to establish in my class.'

'Yes, Miss.'

'And whether, in fact, you want to be in it at all. Do I make myself clear? Sit down. Both of you. One more word out of *either* of you and you'll *both* be sent out. I've had as much as I can take. I swear, do not speak even a single word. For the rest of class, not a single word is to be uttered by either one of you.'

'I need me book, Miss.'

'Chan*telle*! I'm telling you, a vein is about to burst in my head.' She threw Chantelle's book at her and slumped back down behind her desk, rubbing at her temples.

They worked in silence, going on to the next chapter, but after a few minutes Chantelle wrote, *Fanx I ☺ U !* on the palm of her hand and held it out for Niki to see.

# FOUR

'You're not going out again, are you?' Robert said, looking up from his crossword clue. *Deliberately under canvas (6).*

'I shan't be long,' Angela replied.

'Where are you going?'

'To visit Mum.'

Robert knew his whiny voice irritated her, but he couldn't help himself. Since they'd arrived last week, Angie had barely spent five minutes with him. He had told himself that once Nikita started school perhaps he'd get a little more attention, but other than their brief conversation this morning, Angie had hardly spoken two words to him; she'd read a magazine over lunch.

'You'll be needing one of these,' he said, moving towards her with a plastic bag.

Angie frowned at him with such a look of distaste that Robert hesitated mid-step, arm held out in front of him dangling the crumpled bag.

'For your knees,' he explained. He had meant it sympathetically, he wanted to say.

Angie snatched the bag from him. 'I'll be back for when Niki gets home.'

Robert sat back down and started writing. *Intent.*

♠♠♠♠

When he had seen Angela standing back in her room at the beginning of last week, Robert had needed to leave before he began to cry. He cried easily these days, ever since Betsy had gone – loudly, with his mouth hanging open, his chest heaving, until at last he would give a raggedy sigh, blow his nose and get back to whatever it was he'd been doing. Sometimes he wandered around the house making his wailing noise, a sound to fill the empty rooms. He could hardly go around talking to himself.

He'd have to remember not to do that now, remember he had company – people actually living in the house after four years of being on his own. And not just 'people'. Angela. Angela was home. Angela whom he had barely seen since the baby had been just six months old and they had moved out. And then she'd gone completely.

'She's gone, you know. We might never see her or Nikita again.' Betsy had stood in front of him in the kitchen while he ate his cereal. His mouth had been too full of cornflakes to reply. Milk was making its escape out of the corners of his lips; he could feel a thin trickle dribbling down to his chin.

'Are you happy now?' she had said.

But he just sat there chewing up this papier-mâché ball in his mouth. Chewing like a fool. He knew she would think his chewing was an act of defiance. She would take it as his not caring about their only child.

'What was I meant to do, spit it into my bowl?' he asked himself aloud whenever he replayed this memory. 'That would have *really* upset you.'

So he'd kept on chewing, resigning himself to her thinking he was callous – a heart brown and shrivelled like a rotten tooth. But she thought it already by then. Even if his mouth hadn't been full of cornflakes she wouldn't have thought differently at that stage. The damage had been done. He was nothing like the man she'd married.

'Where's the man I married, hey? Where's he gone?' she'd whispered that night, months earlier, thinking him asleep. He'd turned away from her in bed and clicked off his light while she was mid-sentence. She had been explaining why she hadn't told him about Angie's pregnancy. He lay with his back to her, pretending he was asleep, deliberately making his breath slow and loud, even inventing the odd murmur for extra authenticity.

Where was the man she'd married?

Where was the woman *he'd* married, he'd wanted to hiss. To *lie* to him like that. To keep from him the fact that his daughter was *pregnant*!

He still thought of Angela as that child running round in the back garden, dragging behind her a yellow spade that was the same height as she, her hair in pigtails tied with sky-blue ribbons.

Or Angela in her gymnastics competitions, catapulting herself over the horse while he looked on, heart in his mouth.

What did his wife think of him that she would keep a secret like that? And she was wondering where *he* had gone.

'Because I knew you'd get upset. That's why I didn't tell you.' He could hear her voice as plain as day.

When he was thinking these things, having these conversations, he liked there to be space behind him in the room. That way he could pretend she was standing right there behind him.

'Robert. Are you listening? I knew you'd get upset.'

'Upset! That my *fifteen* year old daughter was having a baby! Why would that upset me? How un*reas*onable!'

'Oh, do stop *shouting*, Robert. This is exactly what I mean.'

He wished he'd explained to her at the time. It wasn't so much their daughter's being pregnant, although any father would be horrified, surely – a single mother by the time she turned sixteen. He was a teacher in a secondary school, though – he knew these things happened. No, what had crippled him with fury was the deceit. Suddenly he'd been forced to face the fact that they were no family at all.

And now this baby, the cause of so much upset, was here, grown into a girl. Had fourteen years really gone by? Like all of them these days, she looked to him to be going on at least sixteen, especially with her new hairstyle. Oh, yes, she really looked the part.

He was familiar with girls her age. Strutting along the street like they owned the place. Walking right out in front of cars as if death would never dare touch *them*. So *rude* to shop assistants and supermarket security guards! Throwing penny sweets about in the local convenience shop. Actually *throwing* the sweets at the man behind the counter! How *dare* they! They scared him silly. He'd heard enough about happy slapping to know it was best to stay in once the schools finished each day, go to the shops and post office in the mornings, always be home by three.

It seemed to him girls were worse than the boys these days, what with their raucous screeching, their spitting, and the way they sucked on those lollies. Either they had no idea how suggestive it looked, or they knew precisely.

But she had asked to call him Grandad. 'Shall I call you Grandad?' she'd asked.

If you want.

'Was that really all you said? "If you *want*?"'

'Oh, do be quiet,' he said, turning round before he remembered that Betsy wasn't there. Shaking his head at his foolishness, Robert walked upstairs.

Very slowly, he pushed open the door to Angela's bedroom. She was still living out of her suitcases, clothes spilling out onto the floor. Messier than her own daughter. Obviously not wanting to move in, to accept this place as home.

With a heavy sigh, Robert straightened the duvet on her bed, patting out the creases, and sat down.

'I was thirty-nine when I met your mother,' he said quietly. 'Too old to be pulled into the let-it-all-hang-out culture of the swinging sixties. Father was still alive, so there I was, still living at home in the same house that I'd been born in. . . How could I be into free love and endless parties when I came home from teaching Maths all day and needed to cook Father his tea? Then we'd watch *Z Cars* and I'd help him have a bath and get into his pyjamas. Not what you'd call Rock 'n' Roll, was it?' He gave a little laugh. 'Father used to say the same thing to me every night as I tucked him in. "Where's Mother, then?" he'd say, and I'd reply, "She's not with us any longer, Father, remember? It's just us now." And he'd look right at me and say, "What you need is a clip round the ear."' Robert laughed and shook his head in amusement.

'Your mother tried to drag me along to parties, of course, but I claimed I was too old. Far too lively for the likes of me, I'd tell her. I played the older-man card well. Her friends were impressed, would giggle shyly as though I was intimidating, you know, aloof. Really, I was just shy. I think Betsy mistook it for being masterly or austere in perhaps the way of Mr Rochester, or, I don't know, a tame Heathcliff.

'Oh dear, she – at twenty-eight – assumed she was

left on the shelf! That's how it was in those days. That's how I stood a chance. Eleven years her senior. I kept worrying that I'd be found out, you know? But also, Angie, well. . . I suppose that I didn't want to disappoint her. She inspired in me the confidence she craved for me to have. I could see her desire for a reassuring presence in her life, so it wasn't . . . it wasn't a betrayal or anything. No, I was just trying to be the answer she was looking for. To be that ideal man. Does that sound ridiculous?'

He got up and started to fold her jumpers and stack them on a chair. But then he thought she might not like the thought of him having been here, so tried to put them back as he'd found them – in a heap on the floor.

He thought back to his vain attempts to be manly for Betsy's sake, to fill that void in her life. Betsy's father had been killed in a motorbike accident when she was ten. He had collided head-on with another motorbike. 'They broke exactly the same bones,' she told him, 'only opposite, if you see what I mean. They had the same crack in their skulls.'

She had lived in nurses' accommodation at St George's and visited her mother once a fortnight. Both her younger sisters were married. Her mother had convinced her that she would never marry because she was too caught up in her nursing. Her life was mapped out as one of spinsterhood, to which the entire family was resigned – Betsy included – and suddenly there had been Robert, a father-figure to take her down off the shelf and tenderly brush off the cobwebs.

They married in July 1969, nine months after having first met. Betsy's mother had bought a hat in the January sales, four months before Robert even proposed.

'Six years we waited for you,' he said to the photo of Angela coming first in a gymnastics competition.

'The first year was fine – happy newly-weds. Betsy helped look after Father with such humour and affection. I was amazed to find my love for her capable of growth.

'"Got me a proper nurse, you have!" Father would say. . . I hadn't seen him smile like that in years. "Come on, Mr Smith, time to take you round the block." And off they would go, arm in arm, for his afternoon stroll. I always came home for lunch, and I hated going back for school in the afternoons – watching them heading off for their walks.

'Sometimes Father mistook Betsy for his wife. "Come here, Doris, give us a kiss." But she didn't mind. She'd just lean over and kiss his brow. "John, my love," she'd say. "Here's a kiss for my John."

'He became a lot of work, of course, towards the end. So we didn't think too much about children. . . And then one day Betsy called me at work. I cycled home as fast as I could, tie flapping about, wind stinging my eyes. It was downhill all the way, but I was still too late. I found her sitting by his bed, holding his hand. She looked up and said, "He's gone."

'In our second year, Betsy's mother started hinting about children. Both Betsy's younger sisters had three each. By the third year Betsy struggled not to cry when friends had babies. By the fourth she cried every time she had her monthlies. By the fifth we weren't talking about children anymore.

'And then it happened,' Robert said, shaking his head in bewilderment. 'Thirty-five years old and suddenly she was pregnant. She flung her arms around me and we turned in circles around the kitchen. "We're going to be parents, Robbie! You're going to be a dad!"'

'Why couldn't you just enjoy it?' Betsy's voice came suddenly, as though just over his left shoulder.

Robert leant his head against the window. The lace curtain meant – he hoped – people wouldn't notice him from the street, but he supposed they probably did. They probably walked past and said, 'That's where the old man who leans his face against the windows lives.'

'Why couldn't you just enjoy it, Robert?' If he shut his eyes he could imagine that she was just about to put her hand on his shoulder. About to come and wrap her arms around him and press herself against his back. It was a long time since anyone had touched him.

When he had seen Angela back in this bedroom those same feelings of fear had resurfaced. All that regret. All those years. She had been gone for so long and it was his fault.

Why couldn't he have just enjoyed it all? Just got on with it, gone with the flow, as they say. Why did he always have to wonder?

'It just seemed so strange,' he said. 'To take over five years to get pregnant – and it wasn't like we did anything different. Six years and then suddenly, just like that, for there to be a baby. . .

'Surely it was natural to have wondered whether you were really mine?'

# FIVE

'Sore eye?' said Angie, not understanding Niki's mumble.

'I *said*, It. Was. All. *Right*.' Niki repeated.

'Oh. Well. That's good then.' Angie raised her eyebrows, waiting for confirmation that Niki's first day had indeed been 'all right'. Niki shrugged.

'Want some of this?' said Robert, putting a plate of cake on the kitchen table.

'Where did that come from?' Angie asked. She'd done all the shopping and knew she hadn't bought it.

'I picked some up. Anything wrong?' Robert turned his back in order to pour the freshly boiled water into the teapot.

'Battenberg's Niki's favourite.'

'Oh. Well. That's good, then.' He tried to keep the smile out of his voice.

Niki let her school bag drop where she was

standing. It fell with a thump onto the floor, the sound of a body collapsing. She poured herself a glass of squash then sat down to cut the cake. Three tea plates sat neatly stacked on the table. Two cups and two saucers, and the glass for Niki's juice. He'd even poured the milk into a little jug, put the sugar into a bowl.

Robert turned round with the pot and held it up towards Angie.

She held up her hands in surrender and sat down. 'Might as well.'

♦♦♦♦

'Don't tell them I called because they'll twig. I'll ring again tomorrow instead. Just mark my words – get some.'

Beatrice had phoned for a catch up with Angela and found herself speaking to Robert instead because Angie was out. He'd been reticent at first but had gradually warmed up. How they had got on to Battenberg, she couldn't remember, but she'd advised him that it was a sure-fire way to befriend Nikita.

'Thank you. I'll get some.'

'It was lovely talking to you, Robert.'

Beatrice had hung up thinking, he doesn't sound so bad.

Robert had checked his watch – two-thirty p.m. If he hurried, there was just enough time to pop to The Co-op, buy some Battenberg and be home again before the schools were out. He couldn't remember the last time he'd eaten anything that looked quite so lurid.

♠♠♠♠

Niki peeled off her marzipan in one long strip and rolled it up like a carpet.

'Eat properly, love.' Angie said.

Day one over. *Day one*. Days and days stretched before her. Each day long and lonely, trying to join in jokes about herself, about her posh voice. Knowing the answers to things she'd learnt in Year *Nine* at St Magda's – and here they were in Year Ten! She was tired of being new and strange for the umpteenth time. She just didn't have the energy – yet again – to make the *effort,* to adapt herself. To shed her skin like those snakes she'd seen on a David Attenborough programme – writhing around with their blank, marble eyes, their flickering forked tongues, twisting and itching until finally that old casing came off and they emerged into the sun, different.

When she'd been younger there hadn't been such a specific list of unwritten laws about what TV programmes you were meant to know, which celebrities were in or out, whether you wore plain or patterned tights, how many piercings were in your ears. Or, at least, the codes had been easier. It had been possible to blag her way through the answers and get the nod of acceptance.

Suddenly it all mattered much more and she knew that she was vulnerable. She couldn't even understand half the things her classmates *said* – they used slang she'd never heard before. Even the way they spoke common words was mumbled and distorted so she had to bend forward like Mrs Munroe and say, 'Excuse me?'

*Excuse me!* They had found that hilarious. 'She says "Excuuuuse me"!!!'

'So, d'you like Bow Wow?'

'I'm sorry?'

'Bow Wow, innit?'

A shake of her head. If she pretended to know who – she presumed it was a who – Bow Wow was then they'd ask why she liked him or what was her favourite song or movie of his. One lie would simply lead her to the next unseen trap – expose her as a liar and make her look even more stupid. She had no choice but to shake her head and let them laugh at her.

'Eeeeeeee! HA ha haaaaaaaaa!' They sounded like donkeys, their opened mouths revealing tongues dyed blue by lollipops.

'No *way*!'

'Where you *been*?'

One promising conversation with Chantelle wasn't enough to shake the feeling that she would forever be seen as a neek – someone to be avoided, sneered at.

She thought back to cuddling Popper at The Grange. Lying in front of an open fire in the sitting room with his head resting in the small of her back as he stretched out and toasted his tummy, whimpering and twitching his feet, chasing rabbits through his dreams. Mrs M's rhubarb crumble. Professor M letting her put tattoo transfers on his hands, him guffawing so loudly that Mrs M had put her head round his study door, asking, 'What *are* you two up to?'

'Niki!'

Niki was brought back from her thoughts to find she'd been squashing her marzipan with her thumb, grinding it into the plate with her elbow sticking up.

'I'm going to watch some telly.' She went next door leaving her cake behind and her drink untouched.

Robert resisted the urge to tell her that *Countdown* had already started, but then paused, cocking his head, when he heard the familiar theme music. He put his unwashed cup back on the table and shuffled into the sitting room. Niki was sitting in his seat, which had the best angle for the television. Still, at least his programme was on.

'So you like *Countdown*, then?'

'S'orite,' said Niki, articulating her new word again.

*Countdown* had been a part of Niki's life for as long as she could remember. Wherever she'd lived, every old person she had ever known had always switched on for *Countdown*. Some of them would sit with stubs of pencils and spiral-bound notebooks, jotting down their answers. One man, Mr Wallis, had an entire collection of notebooks spanning several decades.

Angie cleared the plates in the kitchen and began to peel an onion for a lasagne. She added a dash of cinnamon to the frying pan – something Bea had taught her – listened to the mince crackle and hiss and watched it turn brown as she stabbed at it with her wooden spoon. She wondered how many appeasing lasagnes she'd feel compelled to make before Niki forgave her for this move. She'd helped kit out Niki's room, bought her new shoes, paid for her hair to be done. What more is there? she wondered.

But deep down, Angie realised that these monetary acts didn't make someone feel settled, however much she tried to convince herself otherwise.

School had obviously been a disaster. It reminded her of the fall-out Niki had had with her primary teacher at St Magda's right at the start. It made her want to go in and say, 'Magda's didn't start out perfect either, remember?'

It had taken all Mrs M's powers of persuasion to stop Angie packing up and leaving right then, barely two weeks into the job. Instead, she and Niki had talked things through with the school psychologist, and she had to admit that things had been better since – Niki's nightmares had reduced, and she stopped wetting the bed. She was no longer so haunted by the shadowy presence of half-formed memories. Angie didn't like to see Niki so unsettled again –

she didn't know what might be reawakened.

She looked at the clock and then put her head round the doorway into the sitting room. There they were – like two old dears in a home, she thought. It worried her that Niki liked *Countdown* as much as she did. She actually turned the TV on to watch it. It wasn't something that she rolled her eyes at when Mr or Mrs So-and-so insisted on watching it; no, Niki settled into her seat and tried to work out the problems.

Angie saw her daughter as a marbled mix of old lady and little girl. Mollycoddled by OAPs all her life, she had remained the grandchild to be doted upon, and yet able to talk with them about the war, about their grown-up children, about their dear King Charles Spaniel who was now buried under the pear tree. Old and young, with seemingly nothing of her true age. Just her body growing into that of a young woman, with the rest of her having no clue that it was happening.

Beatrice had told her to be grateful – the proper teenage years would come soon enough. She supposed that Bea was right, but seeing Niki hunched forwards with the same eagerness as Robert, frowning with concentration, made her feel a surge of frustration – no wonder she had found school so difficult.

'Any homework?' Angie asked, then headed back to the cooker. Time for the white sauce. She hated making white sauce – it ended up either too runny or thick with lumps. Still, she could always force it through a sieve if the worst came to the worst, or thicken it with cheese.

Niki sighed and stood up. She didn't have much homework, so it shouldn't take her long. Through the window she saw a hunched, elderly lady battling with shopping bags next door. The woman couldn't keep the garden gate open and walk through with her hands full of carrier bags – it kept swinging shut. She tried to open it with her knee but couldn't seem to push it with enough force.

'I'm just going next door,' Niki called and was gone.

Angie put her head back round the doorway. 'Where's she gone?'

Robert peered through the net curtain. 'She's gone to help Hyacinth.'

'Hyacinth Johnson? Is she still next door? I thought she'd have retired to Jamaica by now.'

'She's talked about going back to Jamaica from the day she moved in.'

'Do you remember how we used to throw all our snails over the fence into her garden?'

Robert chuckled and followed Angie into the kitchen to wash up the cake plates. Something was smelling unappealingly cheesy.

♠♠♠♠

Niki took the bags from the old lady's hands saying, 'Let me help.'

The woman pulled back, staring wildly down the empty street.

'I'll carry them in for you.' Niki realised that this might not reassure the woman, who probably imagined she was trying to get into her home to rob her. 'I've moved in next door,' she added, indicating with her head because her hands were now full.

'What?' The woman drew the word out in a big loop – down and up – giving it extra syllables. 'He *dead*?'

'No,' Niki shook her head, thinking of how she'd thought him dead herself until a little under four weeks ago. 'I'm his granddaughter.'

'Well! Nikita Smit'! Ha' mercy upon me! My, mymymy. Never in arl me lifetime did I t'ink I'd see dis day! I be prayin' for you, chil', since de day you was born and here y'ar standin' in me yard! Oh my *days*! Come in, comeincomein.

'Oh, dear sweet Betsy – she longed for you dat much, she did, she came here talking of you arl de time – and when she see you sometimes she come cryin' to me, "Oh, Hyacinth, that little chil'" she say, God rest her. And you never knew who she was, did you? She said she pretended to not be your grandmammy. "Why do such a t'ing?" I ask, but I don't know she ever really knew why she do it 'erself. Oh, she cry dat much over you – it broke 'er 'eart, dat's what I t'ink.'

Niki followed Hyacinth through the dark corridor into the kitchen at the back. The layout was the same as her grandad's house but there were closed wooden doors between the kitchen and sitting room rather than opened, glass ones, making the kitchen feel much smaller. Everything seemed tatty – a once beige floor that had turned dirty brown, mock-wood covering the cupboards now curling off at the edges. The fridge was covered in magnets of Jamaican maps and flags, photos of children, girls with their heads covered in white ribbons and boys wearing sailor suits. Niki put Hyacinth's shopping bags on the kitchen table and started to unpack them. She began with things that went into the fridge because it was easy to see where they went.

'Honestly, chil', I can't believe me eyes are seein' what dey're seein'! We need tea! I put de kettle on and you gotta tell me arl about why you're 'ere. How can you be visitin' your grandaddy? After arl dese years! An' Angela is 'ere?'

Niki nodded.

'Little Angie! My, dat girl were an angel, arlways such a good girl. Such a surprise o' course when you came along, just not what you'd expect, and your grandmammy were so worried and it all went so *sour*. Dear dear.' Hyacinth shook her head and sucked her teeth. They looked big and false, as if they were too wide for her gums and might suddenly slip.

Niki exhaled and relaxed. Here was something familiar. Here she didn't have to worry about watching the right television programmes. Hyacinth sat back and let Niki busy herself – opening cupboards until she found the right one in which to stack the tins. Putting the vegetables into a rickety three-drawer trolley that stood beside the fridge. There wasn't much shopping to put away, so then Niki sat down at the kitchen table while Hyacinth poured the tea, talking all the time, hardly pausing to hear the answers to her questions.

The house was freezing. Niki noticed that Hyacinth kept her coat on and saw that beneath it she wore at least two jumpers. From their collars Niki could see they were both multicoloured and one of them was run through with gold thread. Her coat was black and white dog-tooth tweed, belted at the waist, fraying at the cuffs and collar with mismatched buttons. Her hair had been dyed black, but showed white roots, combed with oil. She wore enormous glasses which perched on her little face, swallowing it up, making her eyes look like small, black beads.

She had typical old lady legs – bowing out at the knees, frighteningly fragile at the ankles. She took pigeon steps in her court shoes which bulged over bunions. The shoes looked stiff and uncomfortable, but they seemed the universal shoes that old ladies wore in Niki's experience – squat, square heels and always in matt colours of beige or navy. Hyacinth's were beige and heavily scuffed.

'I'm tellin' you, me legs gi' me dat much pain. I wake and dey be painin' me. Sometimes I don't sleep 'cause dey painin' me all t'rough de night, you know? Oh, I tellin' you it hurt me dat much. Sometimes I'm not sure I can make it to Church, but I pray, "Lord, help me get out o' dis bed and go to Church," and he do it, you know? And if I do have to miss a week den someone arlways carl me up and say, "Hyacinth, where you been today?" And dey visit me, dey is so good to me. A real family, you know, 'cause my own son live too far away. He in Peckham and it over half an hour so we don't see each other arl dat much. He say, "Momma, you need to move closer," but I live in dis house for nearly fifty year – from when we move over 'ere, me and me dear husband who pass away nearly t'irty year ago – so I know I never leave dis place. One time I t'ink about going home, *home*-home, you know? But I t'ink now I is too old. I visit some time back and I can't take de *heat*! Imagine dat! Ha! I become English!'

Eventually the phone rang. It was Robert.

'Well, hello, Ra-bert!' Hyacinth called out loudly, looking over at Niki – raising her eyebrows and giving a mischievous smile. 'Yes, she here. Yes. Yes.' Each word was drawn out longer and longer. 'Well, goodbye, now Rabert. And you tell Angela she must come round for tea. You, too. It been a larng time. We must have tea. Goodbye. Goodbye.' She hung up the phone and looked at it for a while. 'He were very sad when your sweet grandmammy pass away. I don't t'ink he ever recover. Dear man. Sometime he go round and his face is like *t'under*! Dear Rabert, dear dear. Right, chil' you must go do some homework, eat your supper.'

'What are you having for supper?' Niki asked.

'Me? Oh, I open up a little tin of something. A little soup, that's me. I eat like a teeny little bird, peck peck peck!' She bunched her fingers together and tapped at the palm of her other hand like a pecking beak.

'Why don't you come round?'

'Oh dear me, no, chil'. One t'ing at a time. It very good to see you. You must come often, but me go round? Oh, no, dear girl.'

♠♠♠♠

The lasagne was dry. The cheese in the sauce had made a greasy layer on top that Angie had to spoon off. Not her best. She blamed the electric oven. The pasta had overcooked at the edges and was chewy. Niki twisted some between her teeth with her fingers.

'Eat properly, love.'

Robert worried about what the cheese would do to

his digestion. He could feel it balling up in his insides, solidifying into one heavy lump. He knew it would give him wind and that he would be kept awake. He should have asked Angie to buy some prune juice.

Angie cut her lasagne into neat squares and chewed slowly. It was the cheese sauce that had ruined it. She bit into a lump of flour. How could she encourage Niki to make friends her own age? The first friend she seemed to have made in Tooting was a seventy-year-old Jamaican woman.

She watched Robert swallow a mouthful of food like it was wrapped with barbed wire. Ungrateful sod. This lasagne was a disaster. This whole move was a mistake.

# SIX

Science was Niki's first period on Friday, at the end of what had felt like a very long week. She'd hardly seen Chantelle since her first Maths class – just catching a glimpse of her in the corridor from time to time. Chantelle would grin and wave. Sometimes Niki heard people walking with her say, 'Why you wavin' to dat neek?'

'Ah, she's all right,' Chantelle would reply. 'Saved me skin wiv Hennessey.'

They'd sat next to each other again in Maths yesterday.

'So, what's it like 'avin' a killer as a dad?' Chantelle had asked.

'I don't even know him,' Niki said. She didn't say that growing up she'd had persistent nightmares, had to sleep in the same room as her mum, wet the bed until she was ten because she was too scared to walk to the bathroom at night. She just shrugged, then joked, 'It's probably about as glamorous as having a dad in a mental hospital.' She was relieved, and surprised, that Chantelle hadn't told anyone.

♦♦♦♦

Niki had adopted a tactic of arriving at her classes just before they started. That way she didn't fall into the danger of sitting in someone's place by accident. It meant she was becoming used to sitting next to Sangeeta, who always seemed to be either on her own or with a couple of other Indian girls who all had the same lustrously brushed hair and neat gold studs in their ears.

Walking into her Science class now, Niki saw Sangeeta look up expectantly when she arrived, shifting her books as a show of making room.

I am obviously a friend now, Niki thought. She didn't mind. Sangeeta was quiet and got on with her work – a sort of companionable silence that meant Niki usually got a lot done. They'd asked a few polite questions of each other, but mainly concentrated on the class. Niki wondered if she could get some banter going the way Chantelle did, firing off personal questions without a second thought. But they just smiled at each other and the lesson began. The longer Niki left it, the harder she found it to think of anything to say.

As the final bell rang, Sangeeta said, 'You can come round to my house, if you like.'

'Oh. Right. That'd be good.' Niki nodded and smiled. Her first invitation to someone's house. 'Thanks,' she added. 'Where d'you live?'

'Vant Road, do you know it?'

Niki shook her head.

'It's not far from here. We can walk together, then you'll know the way... Just... There are a lot of people in my house, so don't be surprised, OK?'

'OK,' said Niki, without really understanding. They walked towards the door, but then Sangeeta stopped and turned to face her.

'I mean – it's a flat. But we live there with my family and then my uncle's family, and also my grandparents.'

'Wow. How many people's that?'

'We're nine people,' Sangeeta said fingering the textbook she hugged to her body.

'Wow,' said Niki again. 'It must be a big flat.'

'No. That's the point. It's a two bedroom flat. My family have one room, my uncle's the other and then my grandparents have the front room.'

'. . .Wow.'

'You mustn't tell anyone,' Sangeeta said.

'No.'

'So . . . do you still want to come?'

Niki nodded. 'Yes. I'd love to.' She smiled. It seemed no one in Tooting had a life that would have fitted in at St Magdalena's.

♠♠♠♠

'I told Angela I had a hospital appointment,' Robert confided to Betsy's headstone. 'Well, I *am* quite near the hospital.' He smiled, and leant forward with his trowel to burrow a space for another bulb.

'These daffodils will come up a treat in the spring. Crocuses first, little beaks of white and purple, then the daffs as bright as lemons. . . It's a pity there isn't a Best Kept Grave competition,' he mused. 'Maybe there is. I can just picture that gardening presenter kneeling by graves and rating them. That one with the froggy grin and flyaway hair. You always enjoyed watching him, didn't you?'

For the late summer he would plant some crocosmia to come up; orange was Betsy's favourite colour.

'Red is sexy, daring,' she'd once explained, 'but orange knows how to laugh at itself.' He had replied that she was very odd, and she had squeezed him round the waist and said, 'That's why you love me.'

Digging, scraping at the dirt like this, putting his hands in to straighten a bulb and pat the soil back around its fragile tip – these were the sort of movements that reminded him of caring for Betsy when she became really ill. Plumping her pillow, sliding in a hot water bottle and tucking the sheets nice and tightly around her, plucking a stray feather from her nightie. She had been his own little flower that he had tended night and day, watering, feeding, making sure she got enough sunlight. That's why they'd had the front porch built, so she could sit in the light but not have a draught – see the world go by. He'd known it would look strange, stuck out on the front of the house like that, and had tried to persuade Betsy to let him build her a conservatory looking over the back garden. But she had shaken her head, pursed her lips in that very definite way she had and said, 'At the front, Robert.'

Of course, it had meant that bow-legged Hyacinth stopped by whenever she saw Betsy sitting there. Robert would busy himself somewhere in the house for that hour and all he'd hear would be Hyacinth's voice.

'Rabbiting away, nineteen to the dozen,' he'd mutter under his breath. Not a peep from Betsy.

He'd hold on for as long as he could – until he felt he would explode and roar at Hyacinth for going on and on like that, tiring poor Betsy out. He'd throw down his duster, or the newspaper, and stride out to the porch, trying to stay calm, trying to keep his voice mild and a smile fixed to his face, all the while constructing in his head an excuse to get rid of her – time for Betsy's bath or rest or medication.

But each time he'd pause in the doorway to the porch. He'd pause because he'd see the smile on Betsy's face. Her head leant against the back of the chair, eyes closed as she listened to Hyacinth.

As soon as Hyacinth saw him she'd say, 'Oooh, dat's me cue, me cue, time to be off. Oh my days, I stayed faaaar toooo looooong.'

Betsy would open her eyes, her smile suddenly gone. 'Oh, must you?'

'Time for your. . .' Robert would say.

'Oh, is it?'

Hyacinth would practically back out of the house bowing, as if Robert were King. It made him feel ridiculous seeing her almost cringing to leave him. Was he really that bad? He would turn to the now tired-looking, unsmiling Betsy and feel like a spiteful old husk of a person. Spoilt everything again.

'You can almost smell the jerk chicken and salt fish when she talks,' Betsy had once said after she'd left. She'd sighed and smiled. 'It's like I get transported to the Caribbean.'

In those last days he had to resist the urge to hug her fiercely whenever he lifted her back into bed because by then she was too fragile, in too much pain. Even when he was as gentle as could be, she would sometimes give a little wince, a sharp sucking of breath, and a wobbly smile. 'I'm fine, I'm fine.'

'One of the beauties of the disorder in the health system,' Robert explained, sitting back on his heels to wipe the headstone with a cloth – brought from home, pre-dampened and wrapped in cling film – 'is that it means I can spend a nice long time here before I'm expected home.'

Nice, too, he suddenly realised, to have someone expecting him home.

♦♦♦♦

It was strange caring for someone who was so independent, Angela found. Her dad had gone off, toddling to his hospital appointment, on foot – 'Not far, is it? I can manage' – leaving her to tidy the house.

She'd spoken to Beatrice only yesterday. Maybe that was why she was feeling at such a loose end.

'Peter wants to know how you're filling your time,' Beatrice had said. 'He's worried you'll get bored.'

'He said all that, did he?'

'Actually he did, thank you very much. Might have taken me half an hour to understand, but that's not the point. He is very concerned for you, that this move works for *you*, Angie. He says you need a vocation.'

'I have a vocation.'

'Don't get defensive, you know precisely what I mean. Develop the skills you've got into . . . well, into a career.'

I just need a project, Angie decided. She walked up to the room that was a shrine to her past. Perfect, she thought. I'll paint over these sickly pink walls and get rid of all this junk.

It had to happen at some point, Angie supposed. There were reminders everywhere if she stopped and let herself think about it.

Here it was: a silver-linked bracelet. Chunky. He used to wear it all the time. She remembered that he had refused to tell her how much it had cost.

It must have got in with her things when her mum had gone round to Damien's and picked up the last of her belongings. She couldn't imagine why he hadn't been wearing it. Perhaps he had been trying to send a message to her, hiding it amongst her stuff so that he'd have an excuse to call round and say, 'Have you got my bracelet?' Had he been inventing a reason to see her one last time, and then maybe, just maybe. . .

But he had never called round to ask for it. Or if he had, her parents hadn't told her. She supposed she'd never know.

'You've got to make it a clean break, love,' Betsy had said. 'If not for you, then for Nikita.' She'd nearly always called Niki by her full name. She'd loved it. Rolled it around her mouth like a boiled sweet – Nikita – letting it hit against her teeth.

There they had been, at Victoria coach station. How she'd managed to carry everything, Angie would never know, but somehow she'd packed up her life and that of her baby's and they'd headed off to her first paid job as a private carer. Miss Crenshaw, a wealthy spinster with four dogs that peed all over the house, cocking their fluffy legs next to pot plants, table legs, health visitors. Miss Crenshaw used to spend entire afternoons combing their pantaloons. She had fashioned herself on Barbara Cartland – getting Angie to help her cake herself with make-up each morning, setting her hair with eye-watering billows of spray and securing a little pink hat with a pin. She had been obsessed with Mills and Boon books, loving the scandal of Angie running away from her lover, clutching a brown baby.

Angie didn't want to think about Damien yet. She balled up the bracelet in her fist and threw it in the bin. Maybe this was a project she wasn't quite ready for. She went downstairs into the kitchen and made some sandwiches for lunch even though it was only 11.30. Usually her jobs were so involved with the people she was caring for – she'd be waiting on them hand and foot, tidying, washing, reading to them, playing scrabble, driving them on outings or wheeling them round the shops, getting guest rooms ready for children and grandchildren to stay for the weekends. There had never been enough time to think about not having many friends. She'd met a few mums at school gates, but that would hardly work now Niki was at secondary school.

She sat at the kitchen table, two cheese and tomato sandwiches on wholemeal bread in front of her, listening to the clock.

♠♠♠♠

Niki knew this was the house they would stop at.

Please don't let this be it, please don't let this be it.

But they did stop. I knew it , she thought.

The gate didn't work – it hung open, tilted on a broken hinge. Litter was scattered across the small concrete space. And, to her horror, they didn't head up the steps to the large front door, stacks of doorbells showing that the place had been divided into flats. Instead they headed *down* steps that were slippery with dark green slimy stuff.

'Careful,' Sangeeta said. There was no outside light – it just got darker and darker. Paint peeled from the door and window frames. Leaky brown deposits streaked the whitewashed walls like a tear-stained face. The bins smelt of gone-off chicken. Sangeeta unlocked the door, pushing it through a sea of takeaway menus, free newspapers and post for tenants long since gone. Niki was immediately hit by the smell of spices that filled the house – cumin, chillies, garlic, coriander. Those were the ones she could make out. Limes, too. She could hear music playing and someone singing over it, loudly, and in a language that sounded made up.

'It's a very dark house,' Sangeeta said.

'It's nice,' Niki replied even though they were still only in the hallway, the feeble light from a naked bulb doing nothing to lighten the walls that were painted ivy green. From behind a closed door Niki heard the buzz of a television – the singing had stopped.

'My grandma is always watching movies. Always love stories. You'll hear her weeping in a minute.'

They came to an open door gushing out the spicy smells and walked into a kitchen clouded with steam puffing up from bubbling saucepans. Sauces spattered like lava lakes and dribbled down the sides of the pans causing the gas flames to sizzle with every drip. The window was white with condensation, streaming beads of water.

'Mother.'

A lady turned around. She wore a navy sari patterned with white thread and over it, a burgundy cardigan in chunky cable-knit. Her hair was pulled back into a long plait. Yellow-gold jewellery brightened her ears and neck and wrists. She balanced her wooden spoon on the edge of a pan to come and greet Nikita.

'Your friend! Lovely! Sit, please sit.'

Niki pulled out a chair and sat down.

'Make her sherbet, Geeta, but you're late – the laundry.'

'Yes, yes.' Sangeeta rolled her eyes at Nikita. 'Laundry,' she said.

Niki smiled and rolled her eyes back.

'Sherbet?'

'Ooh, yes. Thank you.'

Niki remembered the first time her mum had introduced her to sherbet dips. They'd moved to a new village and missed a bus from town.

'Typical,' Angie had said when it started to rain, and then 'typical,' again when she looked at the bus timetable in the shelter and saw they had a half hour wait. The wind seemed to be blowing the rain *into* the shelter, but Niki persuaded her mum to buy them some sweets.

Angie picked up two sherbet dips.

'I used to love these as a kid. You've got to try them.'

The rain stopped and they swung their legs as they

sat on the bus shelter seats, dipping their red lollies into the yellow sherbet and sucking it off so that it zinged in their mouths and made Niki close her eyes with the fizz of it.

But Sangeeta didn't pull out little red and white packets of sherbet dip. Instead, she opened a cupboard and got a sticky bottle of dark pink syrup. Its label read *Rose Syrup*.

Rose syrup? Niki could feel her face wrinkling. *Rose?* The lid crunched over sugar granules as Sangeeta unscrewed it and poured the syrup into the bottom of two tall glasses. Niki thought it looked like cough medicine. She'd smelt enough rose-scented soaps, talcum powders and bathroom fresheners in her lifetime to be pretty sure she didn't want to drink anything that tasted of roses.

And then, she watched, appalled, as Sangeeta pulled out a carton of *UHT* milk. It wasn't even from the fridge. UHT milk was right up there with custard creams and chopped liver in Niki's Most Disgusting Foods list.

The milk sloshed in over the cough medicine and the whole drink became a vivid fuchsia. The sort of bubble-gum pink that girls liked for hair bobbles, but not to *drink*! Mrs Devarajah dropped a couple of ice cubes into each glass and then Sangeeta brought them to the table.

Niki forced a smile. 'Thank you. It looks lovely.'

'You don't have to drink it.'

Niki took a breath, raised the glass and gulped as much as she could in one go.

'Wow! It tastes like strawberry milkshake!'

Sangeeta smiled and drank hers too. They giggled at each other's pink moustaches.

Sitting in the kitchen Niki now understood why Sangeeta came to school with the smell of cumin in her hair. She felt enveloped by the steam engine billows of cooking smells, like her skin would now taste of these flavours if she were to lick her arm. Similar to the way Janaia came to school smelling of chip fat, she supposed, and Chantelle always breathed out the scent of strawberry laces.

'Laundry, laundry, Geeta.'

'Yes, yes, Ma.'

'Well, come on!' She shooed them, clapping her hands in front of her as though herding chickens.

'All *right,* Ma!'

Together Niki and Sangeeta dragged a giant bag – a chequered cube the size of a small pony to Niki's eyes – along the road to the laundrette. It had feeble straps and a broken zip. Sangeeta didn't seem at all embarrassed.

I've always been the girl with the second-hand school uniform, Niki thought, but at least we had a washing machine.

She imagined how she and Akiko would fall about giggling at themselves if they were seen like this in the street, calling each other 'reject', but she sensed that this wasn't something to laugh about with Sangeeta.

Sangeeta had brought her French revision with her so they could test each other on their vocabulary.

'I do things like vocab here because I can move around and still be working,' Sangeeta explained. 'For writing subjects I have to wait until everyone has gone to bed.'

'Sorry? Gone to *bed*? What time's that?'

'Well, it all depends on when the baby sleeps. She goes to sleep early but I'm having to either do laundry or clean the bathroom or change the sheets in my grandparents bedroom, or help in the kitchen or. . .' She waved her hands about in the air, endless spirals disappearing into the distance, reams of chores twisting round her wrists. 'But then by the time we all go to bed it's nearly time for the baby to wake up and have her feed. Or to just wake up and *scream*, you know?' She smiled.

Niki looked at her, aghast. 'So you go to bed, then *get up* and do *homework*? In the middle of the *night*?'

'Well, when else would I do it?'

Niki wanted to say, 'But that just isn't normal!' She wanted to say that children shouldn't have to do all the housework, children needed to stay in bed. Or teenagers – they were nearly fifteen – but that was still young enough, surely, to be allowed to sleep at night? To get up – in the dark – and start doing Maths or write a Biology essay? It wasn't possible!

'The secret is peppermint oil.'

'You what?'

Sangeeta held her wrist under Niki's nose. It smelt of marzipan.

'This is almond. But when I get up at night I put peppermint oil on my wrist. It wakes you up. Helps concentration. Lavender helps you sleep.'

'Riiiight.' Niki helped to fold some pillowcases. 'But in the middle of the night!' she couldn't help saying again after they'd been quiet some minutes.

'I know. . . But . . . don't you understand? My whole family is here because of me.'

Sangeeta went to pay and together they dragged

their cubic beast back along the road, puffing out warm clean breaths through its open zip.

'I'm going to be a doctor,' Sangeeta continued. 'We moved here for me to become a doctor. My father gave up a *good job* to come here. Now he drives a van. He used to run a whole department! Office manager. And here he delivers boxes! He gets up at 5 a.m. every day – *including* weekends – and doesn't come back till after eight. All for me to become a doctor. Don't you see?'

Niki nodded – and then more vigorously when Sangeeta seemed to take her silence as negative. 'I see, I do.'

'It's all right for you.'

'What d'you mean by that?'

'You're from here. It's easy for you.'

Niki had never thought of it like that – had always felt burdened by her past, disadvantaged by always being new and different, but looking at Sangeeta, she suddenly felt very lucky.

'Well, I think you're *amazing*,' she said, and watched Sangeeta's face light up in surprised delight at the compliment.

They walked into the kitchen and Mrs Devarajah was already serving up plates of food – spooning different curries and dhal round the foot of rice mountains. She put them down on the kitchen table in the girls' places saying, 'Sit, sit,' then placed a plate stacked with chapattis in the centre.

'This is Auntie Sita,' said Mrs Devarajah.

In the doorway appeared Sangeeta's aunt – a small Indian lady in a pink, velour tracksuit, jangling with the same yellow-gold jewellery as her sister. She made Niki think of Battenberg. The baby she held in her arms had gold bangles wedged on its chubby arms and gold hoops in its ears. Its short, cropped hair was pulled into an elastic with a flower on it and kohl had been painted along its eyelids.

'And who are you?' said Sita, shifting the baby from one hip to the other. She had a tiny body and seemed swamped by the plump baby, whose round, placid face reminded Niki of a Buddha picture that was in her Religious Studies textbook.

'Nikita.'

'Nik-i-ta. Lovely. I'm Sita, Nikita – *ha!* – it rhymes! And you friends with Sang*ee*ta! You call me Auntie. So, you school friend?'

'That's right.'

'Geeta will be a doctor. Clever girl. She lives the interesting life for us all, no? Me, I never leave the house. We,' she looked over at her sister, 'never leave the house.'

'That's not quite true, Auntie,' said Sangeeta but Sita flicked the interruption away with the back of her hand as if batting a fly.

'Just work with babies,' she continued. 'Babies and our parents – ancient babies.'

Sangeeta's mother tutted, but Sita carried on as though she hadn't heard. 'Babies and cooking. Our job, even, is to look after *other* people's babies! Babies, babies, *babies*! They've gone for tonight, but it's all we do. All through the night with this one,' she squeezed her baby and kissed her neck noisily. 'And all through the day when other fat little babies arrive wanting to be fed and changed and cuddled and *fed*.'

She widened her eyes – thickly outlined in black like her daughter's. Niki gave an awkward smile as Sita's stare grew more and more intense.

'We'll go mad in this house with babies.' She scooped at her pile of rice and balled a clump between her fingers, dipped it in some sauce and popped it in her mouth. Her cheeks bulged for a moment, then the whole ball seemed to be swallowed in one gulp. A snake consuming an egg. Her hair was loose and fell about her shoulders – cut in layers that swung and shone every time she moved her head.

Pantene hair, Niki thought, blacker than seemed possible.

'And you?' Sita continued, now chewing chapatti wrapped around a chicken curry that Niki thought looked suspiciously as though it had spinach in it. 'What do you want to be?'

Be? Wasn't it *do*? Niki wondered. She didn't know what she wanted to be. Happy? That sounded a bit lame somehow. What did she want to *be*?

How can I know what I want to be when I don't really know who I am? she thought. It was like a torch dazzling her eyes.

'I guess . . . an artist?' She said it because she had to say something. It was partly true.

'But that's ridiculous. No, you can't do that,' Sita tore some chapatti with her teeth and gulped at her glass of juice – snapping at it all with her mouth open. 'Art! How can *art* feed your family? Ridiculous girl! You aren't thinking. Don't you like science? If not a doctor, why not a lawyer? That's a good profession. What are you good at? You have to work hard.'

Niki and Sangeeta exchanged glances.

'I see you two smiling at each other, but I'm serious.

Do you want to do *this* with your life? Live in a hovel and cuddle fat babies who puke their white sick all over you?' She blew raspberries into her daughter's neck. 'Not you, of course, boo boo. Not you, dee dee. No, Nikita. You must *think*.'

'Leave her alone.' Sangeeta's mother rested her hand on Niki's shoulder. Her voice had a tired smile in it. She squeezed the ends of Niki's tiny plaits. 'It feels like wool,' she said. 'You will be OK. You are from this country. Even if not quite. It's enough.'

'I've got to go!' Niki said, with the sudden sick realisation of having completely forgotten to tell her mother she wasn't coming home straight after school. It was nearly seven – she'd have been expected home before four.

'I didn't mean to scare you off,' Sita laughed and waved her rice-filled hand over the table indicating all the food. 'Stay. Eat more. Come on, it's dinner time. And we have some lovely sweets for afterwards. Geeta made them.' She reached out and hugged Sangeeta to her side. 'You will save us from this hovel, Ghee-ghee. Ha, my butter girl. Our life will be as sweet as your sweets! Hmm, Geety, you are our ticket. Our visa! To new life, no? To a house with more than two bedrooms!'

Niki hovered by the doorway, willing this woman to shut up so she could leave.

'I speak English well, don't you think? You promise to visit us again?' Sita waved but was already looking away as though having forgotten her, nuzzling her baby who squirmed and wriggled like a fat grub.

Niki felt panic rising in her like the crescendo of a fire alarm. 'Thank you for a lovely time.'

'Thank you for helping with the laundry,' Mrs Devarajah said.

Niki nodded and waved, trying to smile, trying not to overreact to the clammering shout inside her to *go, go, go!*

Sangeeta followed her along the hallway. The television still fuzzed through the closed door they walked past. Niki could see a line of light shining underneath it and heard someone blowing their nose in loud, trumpeting blasts.

She could barely see the steps outside without any light.

'Do you know where you're going?'

'Yep.'

Back at her last school, when she'd gone round to friends' houses, a parent always gave her a lift home. Or her mum picked her up in the Munroes' old Land

Rover. Maybe this was how things happened when you were a teenager in London – no one offered to walk you home, even in the dark.

'See you on Monday,' Sangeeta said.

Inside, the baby had started crying. Niki could smell curry on her jacket, highlighted by the contrast of the late-October air that smelt of snow and metal.

She turned and felt her way up the slippery steps. Everything around her was black. She stepped high one too many times expecting a final step that didn't exist so that her foot came down hard and her leg felt lost.

Down the short path, through the broken gate and onto the street. She pulled out her mobile phone from her bag, which was slung on one shoulder, and turned it on. It bleeped with texts and missed calls. The blue light was a comfort.

*Nikiii, where ARE you?!! Get. Home. NOW!*

She would have called or texted in reply, but listening to the message used up the last of her credit.

Streetlamps cast a nauseating glow across her feet and skin.

Oh. My. Days.

She could hear Chantelle's voice in her head.

It came at the same moment – that voice, the image

of Chantelle's grin – as the desperate thump inside her chest on seeing a group of teenagers turn onto the street just a little way ahead. They were coming towards her. Two boys on bikes, three girls walking. She gripped the strap of her bag a little tighter.

# SEVEN

'I'm going mad.' It was all Angie could say to herself. 'I'm going *mad*. Seven o'clock. Where *is she*?'

Her mind filled with worst-case scenarios. Strangled in an alleyway. Caught by a gang of men in the back of a white Ford van. The sort with grubby back doors on which passers-by write with their fingers, *Also available in white*. High on glue in a supermarket car park surrounded by pasty-skinned boys in parka jackets and that fat Jamaican girl with her oil-slick kiss curls. She waited for the doorbell to ring with such intensity that she kept convincing herself it had, checking more than once through the curtains, expecting to see the police standing there.

Robert walked into the sitting room where she paced up and down, clutching the phone to her chest like an injured kitten. She was ready to snap at him as soon as he opened his mouth.

If he tells me to stop panicking, so help me. . .

'How long's it been?' he asked.

'She should have been home before *four* and it's gone *seven*!' She could hear the panic climbing in her voice. Was she being ridiculous? A little over three hours – but it was so dark outside and this was London. Gone seven. No fourteen year old should be out by herself in the dark gone seven.

'What time should we call the police?'

Angie sank down onto the sofa. So he was thinking it too. No words of 'stop worrying' but, 'when should we call the police?' This was real. This was really happening. Time was of vital importance. The sooner the search started the better chance she'd have.

He covered her hand with his own and she didn't feel resentment. She felt . . . love? Gratitude? Whatever it was, it threatened to soften her into a weeping wreck. She pulled her hand away thinking, it's his fault we're even in this city.

'Let's wait half an hour, then I'll call,' Robert said, getting up to pace himself.

♦♦♦♦

Niki was an easy target, and she knew it. She couldn't help but stiffen and look at them with furtive glances, before darting her eyes back down to her feet. Keep your head high, walk like you're not afraid, she told herself, but her legs wouldn't stop trembling. She was just one of those people. One of those sorts who had a face that said, *defenceless*. She felt as if her heartbeat must be audible, as if her jelly legs were wobbling vibrations that could be sensed all the way over there, under their feet.

'I know 'er.' She heard a boy call out and her heart sank like a pebble dropped in a pond. A cold vanishing. She was left with nothing but an empty chasm in her chest.

'She's dat new girl.' He stood on his pedals, leaning on his handlebars with straight arms. To Niki's dismay, he began to weave his bike across the road towards her. Snaking it closer and closer. Tyrone. She'd seen him with his arms slung round girls – one on each side – walking round school with a whole gang trailing behind him. In Art he had stroked the tip of his paintbrush with his thumb so that black paint sprayed like fine dust all over Sangeeta's still life. And when Niki had snatched his brush out of his hand and called him a loser, he'd just grinned and sauntered off.

The others were laughing behind him and followed with springs in their steps. This would be good.

She stopped. Her mind shouted, *KEEP WALKING*! but she just couldn't seem to get her feet to move. She lifted her foot only for it to do nothing more than shudder mid-air and come back down in exactly the same place – and suddenly she was rooted to the spot as if by nails driven through her shoes. The group formed a horseshoe around her. Earrings, necklaces and teeth glinted under the street light. The girls' sleek hair shone like tar. One had cornrows – a maze so elaborate that the pattern was impossible to follow. Another girl's went into a ponytail high on her head, fanned out like the top of a pineapple, tied with a ribbon. At its base, just above this ribbon, stuck in as though forgotten, was a red, narrow-toothed comb. To Niki it looked ridiculous – a *comb* sticking out of your *head*?! But she was too afraid to find it funny.

Tyrone balanced on his pedals, sawing his front wheel back and forth to keep himself upright, then finally dropping one foot to the ground.

'Yooz in me class, innit?'

She knew she should reply. Speak loudly. Sound unafraid, as though she didn't care. But all she could do was look at him.

'Can't you speak or summink? Eh? What's your problem?'

'You ain't scared, are ya?' a girl asked and they laughed.

'I fink she's scared.'

'She's afraid of us.'

Tyrone wore a powder-blue tracksuit. A girl's colour, to Niki's mind. He had two huge earrings studding his lobes. Big fake cubes of clear plastic. His hair was a little Afro. Baby fluff, but growing. She was sure that if anyone else dressed like him they'd be teased. But she guessed he wasn't the sort of boy to get teased.

'Where you been?' His eyes were slits. He turned his face to one side, angling his chin high, eyeing her with theatrical suspicion. 'I see where you come from. You been to the Paki's house, ain't ya?'

'Yeah, you smell of curry!'

'Yuck!' They were cursing and laughing, waving their hands in front of their noses.

'You love Pakis. Paki lover.'

'She's Indian *actually*,' Niki found herself saying.

'Oh, she *actually* is, actually? You posh cow. Indian? Who *gives* a shit?' And the others fell about laughing.

'Paki lover, Paki lover.' They tried to mimic Indian accents and wobbled their heads from side to side.

Did this really happen? She'd studied racism at

school – the abolition of slavery and black Americans fighting for the vote. They'd taken part in Black History Month in her junior class at St Magda's and she'd written the story of Rosa Parks. Now here she was, listening to these black kids making jokes about Indian kids. Shouldn't they be anti-*all*-racism because they knew what it was like – all stand together, or something like that?

'You're not seriously *racist*?' She couldn't keep the scorn out of her voice. It just seemed so *weird* to hear them saying these things.

Their laughter stopped abruptly and they narrowed their eyes in unison. Niki gnawed at her top lip and wished she could learn to keep her big mouth shut.

'I is not racist,' said Tyrone. 'I just hate *Pakis*.'

The others smirked through their noses, shaking their shoulders up and down, swaying from foot to foot.

'You're sick, blud,' the other boy said admiringly, patting Tyrone on his shoulder.

Tyrone sat back on his saddle, hands on his handlebars as if he were on a Harley Davidson. 'So what you got for us, den?' From his pocket, he pulled out a yellow-handled Stanley knife. He locked the blade in place.

Everyone went quiet. He got off his bike and leant it against the girl next to him, the one with the comb jutting out of her head as though she had impaled her skull with it. All the while, he looked at Niki.

'Give us your bag. And de phone dat is in your hand.' He put on a funny voice, but Niki realised that this was not a good thing. He was in an act. Playing the part of someone prepared to rob a girl and use a knife on her. She stood like a waxwork, her eyes transfixed by the blade.

'Give it now or I slash you and when you drop to de ground we will *stamp* on your *face*.'

*'Oi!'*

To her right Niki saw Chantelle marching towards them, her arms swinging, her whole upper body pitched forwards, hands balled into fists.

'You lay one finger on 'er, Tyrone, an' you gonna *regret* it!'

The others muttered to themselves and looked away as if caught smoking by a teacher. Niki's heart burst up from where it had sunk – somewhere below her left kneecap – and felt as though it might explode out of her chest like a bird set free.

Thank you! Thank you! She could hear music inside her head. Oh, Chantelle!

'Back off, Chantelle, what you doin'?' Tyrone said.

'She's one of *my* girls, innit – so *YOU back OFF*!' Her face was pressed almost nose-to-nose with his.

'*She's* your friend? Dis neek? You jokin' wid me. Oh my *days*! You *playin'*!' He slapped his leg, threw back his head to laugh. The others joined in, but Niki could see that it was all going to be OK. She was safe. Relief softened her body. She felt she might either faint or pee down her legs.

'Listen good, Tyrone.'

'You orderin' me?' His voice was low and hard. He lifted up his Stanley knife again, gripping its handle.

'Don't you point dat t'ing at me, you *fool*. Now listen, I say. Her dad in prison, right, and if he hear of dis he will send people and dey will *mash* you – are you hearin' me? You will be shot in de head.' Her accent had changed like his to clipped West Indian, gone was the London slop, each word was staccato. She held her fingers like a gun up against his head.

Tyrone thumped her hand away. Everyone looked at Niki again.

'Dis true?' Tyrone said. 'Your daddy in prison?'

Niki nodded.

'What he do?' Tyrone's chest was puffed out, his lips pressed forward in a sulky pout.

'He kill people, dat what he do,' said Chantelle. 'Now run away and if you are ever t'reatenin' her again, den, *oh my days,* Tyrone, your life be in *danger*, man.'

They started to back off, Tyrone wheeling his bike backwards, sitting low on its seat, the others moving back with him till they turned and he cycled away standing up on his pedals.

'You watch out, Chantelle,' he called over his shoulder. 'Do not go too far, you hear me?'

'Hey, I just save your *life*, man. I just save you from certain *DEATH*!' she shouted at their retreating backs.

Niki trembled all over. The thought of that hard little blade remained with her vividly. She imagined it slicing open her cheek. She could feel the metal, the sharp, hot pain and desperately tried to push the picture from her mind.

'Oh, Chantelle!' she breathed.

'You all right, Niki? Well, dat were a bit *excitin'*!'

'Thank you soooo much.' She clung to Chantelle, who took hold of her shaking hand and helped her sit on the wall.

'You're OK, Niki.'

Niki could feel the tears welling up. She desperately didn't want to cry.

'Come on. I'll walk you home, yeah?' She prised Niki's mobile from her hand, picked up her bag and coaxed Niki to stand. 'The sooner you home de better.'

They walked in silence for a little while. At one point Chantelle said, 'Dat's my house,' and pointed to one of the more modern terraced houses at the bottom of Sangeeta's road. 'I saw you from my window.'

'Well, am I glad about that?' Niki said. She felt drained of all energy. 'Looks like a nice place,' she added, even though the outside looked as tatty as all the other ones in the terrace.

'Yeah, it's all right. It's a bit of a squeeze, though. I share a room with my *two* little sisters, thank you very much, then my brother has his own room, which just ain't fair, and me mum of course. Still, it ain't bad, I s'pose.'

They kept silent most of the way, Niki replaying the whole scene in her head again and again.

'Why did you help me?' Niki asked as they turned into her road. 'I mean, they think I'm a total loser.'

'Who else am I gonna copy in Maths?' Chantelle said and laughed, giving her arm a gentle thump.

'But, like, I'm not *in*, am I?'

'Yeah, well, I like who I like. I don' run wiv just one

group, you know. An' I don' wan' nobody tellin' me who to like an' who not. So dere. Our mums are nurses, our dads are off de planet, you helped me out . . . you're nice. Different. In a good way. It's as simple as dat.

'I don' wanna be tied to no crew. Dere ain't too much gang stuff 'ere, but dere's a bit, you know. Dey gotta look hard, or wha'ever, to save face. Everyone's in gangs – so dese boys fink it's gotta be done like dat round 'ere too. And the girls hang out wid dem like dey're summink, you know, which just bigs 'em up summink stupid. Dey're all on the same estate, dat lot. And what else dey gonna do in the evenings – sit around 'aving dinner wiv deir parents? I don't fink so some'ow!'

'Are they going to be after me now?'

'No, you ain't got nuffink to worry about, neeky girl,' she smiled at her. 'Honest. You gonna be fine. You get respect for a dad in prison round 'ere. Twisted, ain't it?' She shook her head and laughed.

'But they're only fourteen years old!' It had been a boy her own age holding that blade to her face!

'Tyrone's fifteen, actually. Besides, he been runnin' wiv some of de boys from dat estate since he was, like, *nine*. He a right naughty boy.'

'So, are they, like, your enemies?'

'*No!*' She sounded indignant at the very idea. 'Look, OK, doze guys are my mates, too, get it? Dey're not really into beatin' people up, dey were just 'avin' a laugh back dere.'

'Wow, holding knives to people's faces – they sure know how to have fun.'

'. . . Tyrone's my cousin, all right?' said Chantelle.

Niki didn't say anything for a while.

'Your cousin?' she managed to say eventually.

'Our mums are sisters. We're around each uvver's houses all de time.' Chantelle stopped walking and turned to face Niki. 'So don't go cryin' to your mum, is it? Do you get me?'

Niki nodded, finding Chantelle's face just a little closer to hers than was comfortable.

They were on the street outside her house by now. Niki pointed her finger towards her front door. Lights were on in the front room – it all seemed too far away.

'What do I say then?'

'Just make summink up.'

'He pulled a knife on me, Chantelle. That's not OK.'

'*Everyone* carries knives.' Chantelle thumped her arm and grinned. 'Dis ain't bullyin'! Honest. Tyrone'll be your mate tomorrow. Dey just get bored and dere you were – easy target. And why you've chosen Sangee'a and dat lot to eat your lunch wiv is a bit hard for dem to understand. So what d'you expect? It's not personal!' She shrugged her shoulders and grinned, like this was all obvious.

'Right, so *you* can be friends with whoever you want, but because I choose to be friends with Sangeeta, you're saying I asked for it.'

'Chill, all right. I'm just tellin' you to not tell your mum abou' i'. It just ain't such a big deal as you fink is all.'

Niki shook her head. She felt tired and sick. She wanted to be inside with her mum, curled up on the sofa.

They both turned and saw a police car pull up outside Niki's house.

'Don't tell me dat's for you?'

They watched the police officers, one man and one woman, talking inside the car before getting out unhurriedly.

'Dat is too funny, man! You're home after eight and your mum calls de police! No wonder you so neek!' She thumped Niki's arm again. It hurt. 'Don't worry, I won't tell no one! Oh my *days,* I gonna be laughin' 'bout dis all night, man!' Then her voice went serious. 'But make sure you don't say nuffink to *dem*, d'you hear?'

'I get it. *Sheesh!*'

'All right, all right, don't stress.'

They watched the police officers go inside. Niki saw the side of her mum's face fixed in a look of anxiety as she stepped back to let them in, her skin as white as the knuckles of a clenched fist.

'You'd best go and put your mummy out of 'er misery, poor woman. See you on Monday, baby cakes.'

Niki watched Chantelle walk away, pitching forward and shaking her head, floating her arms out as though pretending she were flying, then slapping her hands against her thighs – laughing, laughing.

It's not *that* funny, Niki thought. Her mum was worried, what was so hilarious about that? Just because she didn't live out of control like the rest of them.

She crossed the road slowly, imagining the telling-off that was awaiting her. Before she'd even turned her key in the lock the door swung open and she was enveloped by her mother's arms, could feel the ribs in Angie's back rising up and down as she gasped with relief.

'Where have you *been*? Oh, Niki!' They stood embracing, both shaking and hugging each other.

Niki opened her eyes. Over her mother's shoulders she could see the two police officers in the doorway to the sitting room.

'You gave your mother quite a fright,' said the man, his face composed in a blank expression, weary at having his time wasted.

'I got lost,' Niki said.

'Why didn't you *call*?' Angie stepped back from her, gripping her shoulders with both hands.

'I didn't have any credit.'

'I was going out of my mind.'

'I'm sorry.'

'In future, you come *straight home*, do you hear me?' Angie looked at her daughter's expression. It brought back memories she'd been burying for a long time now – this face of her daughter's, quietly suppressing so much, as if holding her breath in an effort not to cry. She drew her back into her arms, pushing Niki's head down onto her shoulder and kissing it again and again. 'Thank God you're safe.'

♦♦♦♦

Robert hovered in the doorway, unsure what to do. He went and ran the cold tap, filling a glass of water for Niki, carefully wiping its base with a tea towel. When he brought it through both she and Angie were sitting on the sofa, clutching each other's hands. As he gave it to her, he briefly rested his hand on her shoulder. Just a small touch. The first time since she'd arrived that he'd actually touched her. He let go quickly, worried that if he didn't then he might start sobbing. His heart couldn't take such worry.

Robert had actually had many nights like this – twitching the curtains, wondering, where is she, where is she? Always imagining the very worst. The number of times he had planned Angie's funeral in his head was, he knew, ridiculous.

In her mid-teens, Angie had started staying out late – straight after school and on into the night, leaving them with no idea of where she was. And there hadn't been mobile phones in those days. All he could do was make sure she was stocked up with twenty pence pieces for the phone boxes, which, he might add, she'd never used.

It got later and later. She'd arrive home eventually, but he couldn't sleep before she did. It began to affect his concentration in the classroom. He'd lie awake in his paisley pyjamas staring at the ceiling, desperate to hear her key in the lock.

♦♦♦♦

'Are you all right?' Angie asked.

Robert realised that he'd been thinking these things while standing aimlessly in the middle of the sitting room, staring down at mother and daughter nestled together on the sofa.

'Oh. Er,' he had to clear his throat for anything coherent to come out. 'Would you like some dinner? You must be starved.'

Niki shook her head. 'Actually I'm not hungry.'

'How about some cocoa?'

She nodded.

'Angela? Cocoa?'

'Not for me, thanks, Dad.'

'I could bring in *your* dinner on a tray – you haven't eaten a bite.'

'Neither have you.' Angie smiled at him – actually *smiled*. He nodded his head as though he were pointing it out to Betsy. He must remember not to do those sorts of things.

'Listen, love,' said Angie. 'How about you go have

a shower, get in your PJs and then come down for some cocoa under a blanket. We'll watch some telly, how about that? There's probably a good film on, in fact. Dad, have you got the paper?'

'I'll go take a look.' He found the paper on the sideboard in the kitchen and shouted through, '*Sense and Sensibility* starts on Four in *fifteen* minutes!'

He heard Niki thundering up the stairs to get ready in time for the start of the film. He put Angie's food in the microwave to re-heat and began to lay up a tray for her and another for himself. He decided to make Niki some toast and honey, just in case she changed her mind about not wanting to eat.

He knew it had been his responsibility, he thought as he sawed away at the white bloomer Angie had bought. He should have taken the lead over setting boundaries. But instead, he and Betsy had retreated into their respective silences, like snails into shells.

Increments, that's how it happened – by degrees. So subtle that it happened before you even realised. You simply didn't notice and then *bam!* you looked up to discover that change had taken place on a monumental scale. And by then it was too late.

Well, actually, it hadn't been too late for him and Betsy. When they found out about her cancer, all of that dry, encrusted hostility had crumbled to the ground. They had clung to each other with a freshly-emerging love. He still cursed himself for all those wasted years, that decade of silence. What had he been *thinking*? To waste so much time with the one he loved. To jeopardise the love of his little girl.

So much regret.

It was true – it was the things you *didn't* do that were the worst. The things you didn't do, or the things you didn't *say*. Innocuous gestures that on their own seemed harmless – maybe even a little dull – and so were easy to omit. That smile of thanks for your dinner. That hand held and given a secret squeeze before it's let go. That word – hello. Insignificant on their own. What does it matter if one is missed? And yet. The accumulation of not doing them – well. . . It was like playing a piano piece and being too lazy to stretch for the base notes. On the surface it was still sort of all right, but after a while you began to notice their lack. You were left with a sense of something unsatisfying, something incomplete.

That had been their life for far too long. And he had been the instigator. That dryness that had existed between him and Betsy, between him and Angela.

Betsy and Angie – together they'd been fine. No, it

had been in relation to him. His refusal to relate to them. His absence.

And it was – he knew – far more because of all those things that he didn't do, and even more because of all those things he didn't say. Those things he didn't confess. His fear that Angie wasn't his. His fear that Betsy would always feel that she'd settled for second best when she married him, that she'd been tricked somehow and that he didn't live up to her expectations. If only he'd shared these fears. *They* had led to his withdrawal, little by little. His disengagement from their family life.

His trays were ready now, napkins laid under the plates to stop them from slipping, another napkin folded to the side underneath the knife and fork. A glass of water in the top right hand corner. Niki's toast and cocoa.

Yes. Those absences were far more responsible for the chasm that had existed throughout Angela's life than the one thing he *did* do. The one regretful action that continued to tear his heart.

And even now, it was the *not* confessing that continued to cripple him.

# NINE

That night Angie dreamt she was running up stairs. Endless flights. She gripped the peeling white banisters that looked down to an unlit hallway. She could hear herself panting, feel her pulse pounding in her head. Under her arm she squeezed a child too tightly. Squeezed it as if she were eking the last breath out of bagpipes, her lips pressed against its ear, whispering, 'shhhhhhhh' and then running, running, up the never-ending stairs, running, running, until her thighs and calves burned.

She woke to find herself clutching her pillow, her nightie damp with sweat, panting as if she really had been running. The moon was a sliver seen through the gap in her curtains. She lay still for a moment letting the rise and fall of her chest calm, then threw back the covers and went to the bathroom to splash cold water on her face.

Her pale, sleepy-eyed reflection in the mirror

above the sink looked gaunt. Surely thirty shouldn't look this old? Being in this bathroom each morning brought everything back – it was where she had taken her pregnancy test fifteen years ago.

Niki had been trembling last night when Angie held her in her arms – actually *trembling*. She couldn't bear to think of her little girl wandering those streets like that – terrified, vulnerable. Even though she was back safely, all Angie could think about was what might have been.

That quiet, gentle face, those alarmed eyes. It had taken her back to Nikita as a baby, gripping her clothes with tiny fingers – fingernails so small they seemed miraculous. Her fuzzy curls, bouncy and uncontrollable. That corkscrew hair had made Angie want to hug Niki every time she turned around and saw her standing there.

'You are so *adorable*!' She'd hug and hug her, swaying from side to side so that Niki's brown little legs and podgy feet in their white First Steps shoes swung to and fro.

Such serious eyes. Seeing more than young eyes should. Not that Niki could probably remember, but still, Angie was sure it was inside her. It must have coloured her somehow. Those nightmares, her dark imagination, all that bed-wetting that had only stopped relatively recently, shivering like a frightened rabbit, her duvet pulled up over her face. Clinging to Angie as though she were suffocating. Those earth-dark eyes staring at her in silent terror. Widening with every new sound from downstairs.

Angie could distinctly remember prising off Niki's baby fingers, surprised at the strength of her grip, sliding her under the bed in the spare room and pulling the duvet down so she couldn't be seen.

'Shhhh. Shhhhhhhhh. You stay here. Quiet as a mouse, OK? Not a squeak. It's all going to be fine. Shhhhhhhh.'

What mother, however young and stupid, would expose her child to such things for so long? So she had been young and afraid – so *what*? What kind of excuse was that, exactly? If she could meet her younger self now. . .

If sixteen-year-old Angela were standing in front of me right now, she thought, so help me I would smash her head against this wall. I would thump my fists into her back for what she was willing to put up with.

It took effort for her not to sob out loud.

She sat down on the edge of the bath and raked her fingers through her hair.

I was so besotted by him, she thought, despising herself for it. He'd driven this great car, had worn great clothes and been *so good looking*. She'd been the envy of her friends.

All her experiences of men and sex until she met Damien had been of the frantic, desperate sort. She had found it all a bit distasteful, if she were honest about it. Pawing at her. Grunting in her ear. Twitching their bodies, their breath coming heavily through their noses. Sometimes she'd had to screw her eyes tight shut until all she could see were red and yellow specks swimming like the patterns of a kaleidoscope.

Just keep smiling and it'll soon be over. *Why* had she given herself so easily – as if it made her grown-up, powerful even? Where had she got these ideas from? That it was all fun with no consequences – that it had no effect on how she would feel about herself. . .

But with Damien it had all seemed so different. In the bar, on the night they first met, he hadn't wanted to go outside with her. No hand had slid surreptitiously round to her bum as they chatted in the crowded room.

He had just wanted to talk, and had bought her a drink.

Then he'd said, 'Well, I've got to be off now.'

'Don't I get a kiss?' she'd asked, looking up at him through her eyelashes. Fifteen years old, sipping her Hooch and letting the tip of the bottle linger on her lips.

He'd smiled, leant in very slowly, and pressed his lips to her cheek. Just touched them lightly, dry and soft, the way a son might kiss his mother.

'Bye, Angel-face,' he'd said and was gone, leaving her cheek tingling where he'd touched it. A memory burned into her skin with the gentleness of a leaf falling from a tree.

She had begged his phone number off one of his mates.

He used to pick her up after school, drive her around, music pumping so hard that she could feel the base rhythms pulsing through her chest.

A *stupid* girl playing at what I didn't know.

Thinking I was all grown-up.

This man with his flat, his car, his clothes, his mates. And he'd all that money. . .

The sound of crying made her look up. She walked quietly along to outside Niki's door. It was open; she could see the night light glowing across the floor. Niki was lying just as Angie had been – curled on her side, hugging her pillow.

'Nik-nik,' she whispered.

Niki looked up, surprised to see her. There was no way of hiding her tears – on realising it, her face crumpled again and she reached out her arms towards her mum.

Angie sat down on the bed and stroked her daughter's hair.

'Darling, what's wrong? *What happened?'*

Niki shook her head into her pillow. 'I just. . .'

'Come on. I'm your mum.'

'I was dreaming.' Niki rolled onto her back to look at her.

Angie wiped away her tears with her fingers.

'I had this dream,' Niki said, 'where I saw my grave.'

'Oh, sweetheart.'

'And the headstone thing was all broken and fallen over, all overgrown. Everyone around me was crawling out of their graves – all grey-green skin falling off them and horrible black mouths wide open, these black, shining tongues—'

'Niki, love,' Angie said, wanting her to stop, but she could see Niki's eyes staring ahead of her, reliving every detail, unable to keep it inside her head.

'They were clawing their way out, their clothes

hanging off them like scraps of skin, and they were all going home to find their families or something. You know, like that horror story about the monkey paw? Where the mum wishes on the paw for her son to be returned to her. But he died in some accident in a factory, so when he returns to her it's with all his horrible injuries and everything, all cut up and missing his arms and stuff. They were like that – wanting to return to their families, but not realising that they would be terrifying.

'I looked down and saw that my skin was the same as theirs – green-grey and rotting. And I'd been sliced open right down my front. It was all open, my insides and my blood had dried up inside me. All my organs shrivelled and hard. . .'

'Niki, you don't have to go on, sweetheart, you can forget this. Let's turn on the main light.'

*When* would she stop having such horrific dreams? Angie wondered, pleading into thin air. When would her imagination leave her alone?

'And I knew I shouldn't go home, that I was too hideous, too disgusting. And then I thought, where *is* my home? I had no idea how to get to any house I'd ever lived in. I sat down beside my grave and wanted to die all over again, but I was too scared to get back into it in case I *didn't* die, you know, in case I would then be buried alive. I just sat there, dead but not dead, too afraid to get into my grave, but with nowhere else to go.'

Angie sat back down on the bed and stroked Niki's hair thinking, this is all my fault.

'I'm scared of dying,' Niki said.

'No one's going to die.'

'*Everyone* dies.'

Our life has overshadowed her with death and frightening memories, Angie realised. All those frail people she's seen fade away, watching them wrestle with fears of life coming to an end. Our constant moving from place to place, looking over our shoulders. All those questions I've never properly answered for her.

'Do you believe in heaven?' Niki said. 'You know, like a safe place where we get to live forever and it's all perfect?'

'That's what Grandma believed.'

'But what about you?'

'Sweetheart,' she tucked Niki's hair behind her ear, smoothed her hand over the duvet cover. 'Sometimes,' she said finally, 'when I wake in the middle of the night I feel afraid of dying. Or I have a worry that won't go away. A fear. And I feel terrible despair. *Everyone* feels this way. Everyone. That's what it's *like* – you wake in the night and you feel desperate and overwhelmed.

'But you just need to go back to sleep, darling. Then it's morning and everything is better. Things are never so bad in the morning. This was just a horrible, horrible nightmare.'

These fears, Angela thought, are your own. My little girl. Full of imaginings, full of your own sense of self – seeing everything through separate eyes. I can't protect you from this fear or any other. I can't save you from danger.

'Shall I stay?' she offered, as much for herself as for Niki.

Niki nodded pulling back the duvet for Angie to climb in next to her.

'How about Grandad? When's he going to. . .?' Niki whispered.

'I honestly don't know. He won't tell me.'

Niki began to cry again, pressing her face into her mum's shoulder.

'*Shhhh,* come on now, Niki, love. You just need to get some sleep. You had a shock last night and you've woken from a nightmare. You'll feel much better if you just try to sleep.'

'We've only just met him.'

Angie kept stroking Niki's hair until she felt Niki's fingers twitching intermittently as though tapping Morse code, and she heard her breath come deeply from a place of utter peace. Rest. Angie hoped that was what death was like.

*We've* only just met him. In many ways Angie supposed that was true. She had barely known him while she was growing up and then hadn't been in contact with him for thirteen years – except for at the funeral.

Her own father. About to die. And she was only just meeting him.

♦♦♦♦

Angie woke while it was still dark outside. Niki had rolled away from her to face the wall, taking the pillow with her. Sliding out so as not to wake her, she headed to her bedroom, found her slippers and ancient towelling dressing gown, and went downstairs.

Robert was already up, also in his dressing gown and some paisley pyjamas that Angie recognised from her childhood.

'Those are never the same pyjamas,' she said

picking up the kettle to fill it with water.

'I've had these . . . I don't know, ten years, twelve?'

'They're exactly the same as your old ones!'

'They're from Smith Brothers. I have to admit, I don't particularly like paisley – burgundy paisley, of all things. No. But for some reason your mother kept on buying them so, what can you do?'

'And you never told her?' Angie laughed, pausing to look round at him.

He shook his head, bending over the cup of tea that he was nursing between his hands. She could see a little smile turning up the corners of his mouth.

'You are. . .' She stopped smiling and turned to face him fully, hugging her arms around herself. 'There you were, this strict "Maths-Teacher-Dad",' she held up her fingers to indicate quotation marks, 'and now I hear you were this ultra-sensitive husband who couldn't bear to tell his wife he didn't like the pyjamas she bought him throughout their married life.' She gave a disbelieving laugh – a snort of breath that was exactly what Betsy used to do when she was unconvinced by something.

'We had good times, too, Angie,' Robert said in a quiet voice. 'Don't you remember our gardening? Going to your gym competitions?'

Angie turned her back again at the sound of the kettle finishing its boil. She stuffed a teabag into a mug, sloshing it over with hot water.

'Don't you remember our holiday in Devon where Mum and I had been for our honeymoon?'

'Yes, we had good times, Dad,' she faced him again and Robert did his best to keep looking at her. 'But you were so changeable. We'd be having this great time, digging giant moats against the tide, tying the sweet peas to their canes, whatever, and then suddenly your face would change and you'd become Maths-Teacher-Dad.'

Had that been her name for him – Maths-Teacher-Dad? There was something in its dullness, its lack of imagination, that seemed to make it even more hurtful. Would he have to tell her, he wondered. Would that be the only way for her to understand the way he had been? Those sudden pangs of regret or uncertainty over what he'd done, over who Angela really was – *his* daughter? And suddenly it would be as though a raincloud had moved right over him – everyone else continued to play in the sunshine while he was stuck in shadow. He would look over at Betsy and wonder. Or else he would remember the other thing, the worse thing –

the thing that remained when he realised that Angie had to be his, she looked just like him. That was when it became really bad, that was when he would look at his wife and daughter and think, what have I done? and he just couldn't bear himself.

'And then you became permanently this serious, distant figure who hardly said a word.'

'Around the time you went completely off the rails.'

'What a coincidence.'

She slammed the door to the fridge unnecessarily hard but he managed to stop himself from saying anything.

His changes had simply become too frequent. Betsy had tried her best, he knew that. But there came a point when he'd hurt her too many times with his withdrawals and coldness. She had withdrawn herself and suddenly he was stuck. There was no one to pull him back into the sunshine.

'I'm taking my tea upstairs.'

'Your mother forgave me. Can't you?'

But he wasn't sure she'd heard.

♦♦♦♦

Niki lay in bed until mid-morning. She heard her mum go through to the shower, and the slow tread of her grandad hauling himself up the stairs to take his turn.

She heard him say, 'Isn't she up yet?' and her mum replying, 'She'll get up when she's ready,' in a snappy voice. She heard the front door slam and then open again an hour or so later. The sound of her mum with supermarket shopping – the rustle of plastic bags, cupboards opening and closing as she put everything away. The smell of coffee and toast.

Niki ate her breakfast in her pyjamas – Angie had got her Coco Pops as a treat and she ate two bowlfuls, each time almost overflowing the brim.

'Darling,' Angie sat down purposefully at the kitchen table and held out her hand for Niki to take.

Niki put down her spoon and looked up.

'I am so glad that you're safe. But we must learn a lesson from last night, OK? I'm not telling you off, love, but you must come *straight home* from school. You mustn't try any new routes that get you lost. And if you *are* lost then you go into a shop, or a restaurant, and you *ask* someone, OK? You ask to use a phone. Do you understand?'

'Yes, Mum.'

Angie stood up and kissed the top of her head.

'Look, OK, I wasn't lost.' There was a voice inside Niki yelling, 'No, don't say it!' But she'd begun now.

Angie sat down.

'Go on,' she said.

'I went to Sangeeta's house and I forgot to tell you I was going and then I'd run out of credit and so then I came home but it took longer than I expected and it was dark and I was really scared, but then I saw Chantelle and she walked me home but we got here and the police had arrived already and I'm *sorry*.'

'Oh, *Niki*!'

'*Sorryyyy!*'

Angie blew out a stream of air. 'Well, at least you're safe, but *honestly*, love.'

'I *know*.'

'I suppose the amount you scared yourself is probably punishment enough, but really I feel like I should ground you or something.'

'That's so American.'

'Well, you can't just be going *off* like that! You should have used *their* phone. I don't even know who this Sangeeta girl is – I should speak to the parents before you go round to anyone's house. I thought you were smarter than that.'

Niki didn't know why she'd felt the need to tell her mum what she did – it wasn't even like it was the whole truth. But somehow telling her something a little closer to the truth made it seem less like a lie. She almost believed it herself.

Later that afternoon Niki went with her mum to buy a DVD from The Co-op. She bought one about a white ballerina girl falling in love with a black hip hop boy. She'd seen it already, but it was on offer and it was the sort of film she could watch again and again.

Litter whirled in the autumn winds, swept into new swirls by buses shooting past as though their brakes had failed. There weren't many shops that interested either of them, so they walked back towards home. It was already getting dark and had only just gone four o'clock.

As they got near the turning into their road, Niki saw Tyrone walking towards her. He was trailing behind his mother, dragging a tartan shopping trolley.

'Tyrone! Hurry *up*!'

His little sister was holding his hand.

He looked up, saw Niki and quickly dropped his sister's hand.

*'Hey!'* she squealed and grabbed his hand again.

Niki found herself having to squash down a smile

as she saw him muttering to himself and looking down at his trainers.

As they passed by each other Tyrone looked up.

'Hi, Niki,' he said.

Niki was going to walk past, but Tyrone, who'd dropped his sister's hand again, reached out and took hold of her wrist. Angie had walked on a couple of steps, found Niki wasn't with her and turned, raising her eyebrows in a questioning look. Tyrone gave Niki a sheepish smile.

'You OK?' he asked.

'What? After having a *knife* held to my *face*?' she hissed through clenched teeth.

'Look, I'm sorry, yeah. You know . . . about . . . just messin' like. No 'ard feelin's or nuffin.'

'Yeah, right.'

'*TYRONE!* Oh!'

'Oh, man.' Tyrone muttered as his mother started walking back towards them.

'And who's this?' said his mum, sidling up with a teasing smile. 'Hello. I'm Taiyana.'

Niki felt herself cringing as Angie walked back too. Soon the two mums were chatting about their moving back into the neighbourhood after over ten years away.

'No 'ard feelin's, yeah?' Tyrone said again quietly.

Niki shrugged, concentrating on a disk of chewing gum squashed into the pavement, blackened from being trodden under countless footsteps.

'I ain't gonna beg, girl, but I is sorry, yeah? Chantelle's bin at me all freakin' mornin'.'

This time Niki found herself smiling properly. 'Well, that almost gets you some sympathy.'

'Too right.'

'Nice to meet you!' Taiyana was saying, then gave Tyrone a push to get going.

'And you,' said Angie. 'Bye.'

Tyrone pulled a face that was half a smile goodbye, half a dying-of-shame grimace at being caught dragging a trolley with his mother and little sister.

'She was *very* nice,' Angie said afterwards.

Niki glanced back at Tyrone and then hurriedly turned away when she saw him starting to look back over his shoulder.

♦♦♦♦

Once they got home Niki headed round to Hyacinth's.

'You help me make ackee and saltfish patties, OK? I tell you what to do and you do it. I gonna see me son tomorrow and I *arlways* take him deez.'

Niki felt she could listen to Hyacinth talk all day. The sounds of her words were so different. She wondered whether she would have spoken more like that if they hadn't moved away – switching accents the way Chantelle could.

'So, you run away last night?'

'No! Who said that?'

'Your grandaddy gi' me a carl to see if you were 'ere, but I say, no, I not see you fer days. Not nearly arl week.'

'I'm sorry . . . I've had a lot of schoolwork.'

Hyacinth sucked her teeth and bent stiffly to get a tin of ackee from a cupboard. This obviously wasn't good enough.

'I can come round tomorrow, too, if you like, after you get back from Church.'

'Ball up dat pastry now and put it in de fridge while we make de fillin'.'

Hyacinth had boiled up the salt fish earlier – the smell had greeted Niki when she'd first entered the house, but she'd got used to it now.

'I'll chop de chillies, we don't want you gettin' it on yer fingers and den blindin' yerself later.'

Niki fried the onion, garlic, red pepper and chillies,

then began mashing in the ackee and salt fish, while Hyacinth stood next to her throwing in handfuls of seasoning.

'So, where were you den?' Hyacinth asked.

'I went to a friend's and forgot to tell my mum, and got home late.'

'You caused dem dat much worry, nah.'

'I know.'

Hyacinth smacked her lips and shook her head. She was dressed in several jumpers again underneath some sort of house dress. At least, Niki hoped it was a house dress and not something Hyacinth wore in public. It looked like a giant curtain she'd sewn into a tunic – orange cloth with enormous blue and yellow flowers all over it. Niki had never seen anything like it. On her feet she wore fleece-lined boots with thick socks inside.

'In de marnin' I can see me breat',' Hyacinth had confided, but shook her head when Niki suggested she put the heating on.

'So, you get home real late, den?' Hyacinth said, as she stirred the fried mixture, then turned off the gas ring.

Niki looked down at her – Hyacinth came up to about her shoulder.

'A gang stopped me,' she said.

'*No!* When dat happen?'

'When I was walking home. They had a knife.'

'Oh, chil'! What *happen*?'

'It was this boy from my school who had it. One of those craft knives with a yellow handle – do you know?'

'Oh, you poor t'ing! You must be real *scared*. Oh my days.' She sat down heavily, shaking her head back and forth, back and forth.

'But my friend turned up and she got me away.' Niki shrugged. It seemed a long way off now, as though perhaps it hadn't really happened and she had only seen it on TV.

'What your mummy say?'

'I didn't tell her – I can't!' she added, stopping Hyacinth from interrupting. 'They're at my *school*. My life wouldn't be worth living.'

'You can't be bullied like dat, Niki. Dis is no good.'

'It's OK. Really. My friend made it all OK. They won't do anything like it again, because they know I'm, like, I'm all right. I saw the boy today and he said sorry. You know, it was just meant as a game and that.'

Hyacinth tutted and shook her head. 'Game my *foot*. Dere ain't no excuse for *"games"* like dat.'

'Besides,' Niki added, 'they know about my dad.'

'What your daddy got to do wi' it?'

'You know.'

Hyacinth shook her head again, as though the entire world were a mystery to her. She pushed herself out of her chair, pressing down with both hands on the kitchen table to help her stand. Wincing, she hobbled slowly to the fridge to get the chilled pastry.

She threw a handful of flour over the table, pulled off a lump of pastry and rolled it out in a few deft moves. Spinning it round and round on the floury surface between her hands, Niki was impressed to see it end up perfectly round.

'You spoon in de mixture . . . uh-hum, good. And now you fold it over – yes – and now press a fork on de edges, like so. A little pleated edge. Good. OK? I roll, you do de rest, yes?'

They worked together on the patties which Niki then lined up in rows on a baking sheet.

'Deez will be *good*! Keep me son happy, eh?' She smiled and nodded with satisfaction as the rows built up. 'So . . . you seen your daddy den since you come 'ere?'

'No.'

It had never occurred to Niki that she could see him. She supposed the prison must be nearby. She wondered what her mum would think. . . And why, really, would she want to go and visit someone who was a murderer, or who had done something equally bad?

'He's just not in our life, OK, darling, that's how you've got to think about it.' That was all her mum had really said about him and Niki had learned not to ask. He was a bad man. Her mum was grateful that he'd given her a beautiful daughter whom she loved, but other than that there was no place for him.

Should she be thinking about visiting him? Talking to him on one of those phones with a glass window between them?

Hyacinth chewed the side of her lip, nodding with her head low as though her pastry-rolling took a lot of concentration. 'Him being so close, tis a shame. . . But, well, it work out pretty good finally, so we mustn't be too sad about it arl. Dear me, for a while dere it arl go so bad. Dreadful it were fer everybody, let me tell you. . . Still, we gotta be t'ankful dat it arl good in de end. Arl to rights. Yes – for dat I give t'anks to God.'

'How do you mean it's all good?' asked Niki. She supposed they weren't in danger from him, but still, it was hardly a happy ending.

'Well, your mummy being 'ere now – arl grown-up wi' dis lovely daughter,' she grinned her false teeth at Niki and patted her arm. 'And den your daddy, wid his beautiful wife and doze two wee little girls, little angels!

'Dat Dilani – she a *beauty*. . .' Hyacinth's voice trailed off as Niki stood staring at her, a spoonful of filling held out in front of her like some sort of offering.

'You know he married, surely?' Hyacinth said, frowning. 'You know he a daddy again?'

'I thought he was in prison.'

'Prison?' Hyacinth looked confused. 'No, chil',' she said in a low voice. 'He in Croydon.'

Very slowly Niki slid her lump of filling onto the round of pastry. She folded it over with quiet precision and neatly pressed the edges with the teeth of the fork, all the while sucking in her cheeks, holding her breath, blinking her eyes as though the onions were still making them sting.

'He weren't in dere for hardly no time. He a good boy, really, you see, just got into some bad t'ings for a while back den. But 'is family stick by 'im and 'is mamma were prayin' and prayin' fer 'im. An' he *change*.' She snapped her fingers. 'Almost like it were overnight, as far as I 'eard de story. 'E come out o' dere a diff-er-ent man. Back to de smilin' boy we arl knew from way back.'

Niki laid her pattie amongst the regiments of others then sat down as if she, too, suffered from legs that pained her the way Hyacinth's did. She put her elbows on the table, not minding the flour, and rested her forehead against her hands.

It had to be a mistake.

Her dad was a murderer. She'd lived with this fact all her life. He was an evil murderer who haunted her dreams.

'Oh, dear, I'm sorry. I had no idea. I t'ought you would *know* all o' dis!'

'I have to go home.'

'Oh, what have I done?'

'It's not your fault. I'm glad you told me.'

'But what you gonna do? You can't tell your mummy dis.' Hyacinth grabbed her sleeve as Niki stood up. 'Listen to me, chil'. Dis a big *shock*. *Shhhhh*, listen to me. Your mummy don't know deez t'ings.'

'I bet she *does* know. She's lied to me before. . .'

'But what if she not know? Wait! We must t'ink.

Don't rush nuttin'. It not fair to do dis sort o' t'ing just 'cause you feelin' angry. Niki. You listenin' to me? Niki?'

'*Yes.*'

Secrets, secrets, secrets, she thought. It's just another word for lying.

She went home and straight upstairs. She heard her mum shout from the kitchen, 'That you, love?' but didn't answer. She felt as though there was a bad taste in her mouth – a sourness that seemed to even be in her blood, as though she had bitten into something sharp and bitter and its juices had flooded throughout her body.

So there was her dad – the murderer – living in some neat little house only a few miles away. With a beautiful wife and two little girls.

He had two daughters!

Had it never occurred to him to come looking for *her*?

Surely her mum had known. How could she not know? She'd lied about Grandad. She'd lied about Grandma. There was no end to the things she'd kept hidden.

# TEN

Niki carried this knowledge inside her like a foetus in a womb. She could feel it kicking. In everything she did – every sip of water she drank, diagram she shaded, sentence she wrote. Her father was free, her father had a wife, her father had other daughters, beautiful little girls. Her father was a good man.

'You've gone very quiet, love,' Angie said.

*Did* she know? Niki wondered. How could she *not* know? Surely she had known how long his prison sentence was for – had she never wondered if he was out now? How could she have painted him as bad as she had done if he had been out again so quickly? Niki remembered the nightmares she'd had, waking to find her mum stroking her hair away from her cheeks that were damp with perspiration and tears, forever looking over their shoulders for a phantom, this absence that seemed to become embodied precisely because he wasn't talked about, couldn't be seen.

'I'm scared he's coming for us,' she'd whisper.

'He's never coming for us, love – he's in prison. He can never touch us.'

Like some shadow on the wall, looming, coming closer; she had always known – always *believed* – that if he managed to find them, then it would be really bad.

Why have I always thought that – like he was some baddy from a movie – when I can't even remember his face or his voice? There must be a reason why I think of him like that . . . or was it just Mum telling me he was in prison? Is it the way she refused to talk about him, went all stiff and got that look on her face – are all my ideas about him made up?

'How long did we live with Dad?' she asked Angie one evening a couple of weeks later.

'Where did that come from?'

Niki shrugged.

'Well, first of all we lived here, with Grandma and Grandad, for about your first four or six months or so, then with your father for a while, then we moved out of London.'

'How long's a while?'

'What does it *matter*?'

'I was only asking.'

♦♦♦♦

At school she continued to sit next to Sangeeta for most of her classes. They ate lunch together each day, along with a couple of other girls – Raima and Kakali, both from Uttar Pradesh, like Sangeeta, and Nasih from Eritrea whose parents couldn't speak any English.

At times Niki was able to forget about her dad – about all her mum must be keeping from her. When they had their break times together, she could laugh along with them, be silly about nothing in particular.

'You shouldn't hang out wiv dem, you know,' Janaia said to her one day.

Niki hadn't seen much of Janaia or her friends since her first week. It hadn't occurred to her that they might mind; all Janaia had done was show her to the form room on the first day – it wasn't like that had given her ownership.

It was morning break, and lots of them were in their form room where Niki had come to pick up a textbook. Sangeeta and the others waited by the door to go to their next lesson. It was now the end of November; they had all taken to wearing their coats inside. Niki had got a new one from Primark. She had joined the tribe of girls whose hoods were trimmed with fake fur.

'We're gonna need to fink of a new name for ya', neeky girl,' Chantelle had said, yanking the hood up over Niki's head. 'You startin' a look a bit street!'

Niki walked past Janaia and the friends she was sitting with, not bothering to answer.

'I *said*. . .' Janaia repeated, moving to stand in Niki's way as she turned to leave, textbook in hand. 'You shouldn't hang around wiv *dat* lot.'

'I don't care what you said,' Niki replied, causing some of Janaia's friends to make choking noises of disbelief.

'What was dat?'

'You heard me.'

She held Janaia's gaze, feeling the fury of all that was inside her – anger at her mum, confusion about her dad and his beautiful daughters who'd suddenly appeared out of nowhere, his beautiful wife. She'd had enough of girls like Janaia.

Janaia banged into Niki's shoulder again as she went to sit down with her friends, but this time Niki was ready and pushed her own shoulder back into Janaia, causing her to stagger.

'You cow!' shouted Janaia. Her friends stood up to surround Niki.

'Oi! Are you tryin' a 'ave a go, Janaia, you great big

*fat pig*?' Tyrone called from the back of the classroom.

'Oh, leave off, Tyrone,' said Janaia.

'You'd better not touch 'er. She's sick, man, 'er dad'll 'ave ya.'

Janaia and her friends muttered to each other under their breath, and picked up their things to go. 'Yeah, well, we were leavin' anyway,' said Janaia. 'We'll leave you to your neeky *sket* of a girlfriend.'

She marched from the room, shouting *'Boo!'* into Sangeeta's face, making her jump. Her friends cackled with laughter and swung their bags over their shoulders, heads held high.

'You'd better be goin'!' Tyrone shouted after her. 'And you'd better be watchin' your *back*!'

'She's gone, you idiot,' Niki said, moving towards the door.

Tyrone grinned. 'Like yer coat,' he said, but she ignored him.

'Oi! I just saved your *life*!' he shouted, jumping up and running to the door. He held onto the door frame and leant out into the corridor. 'I'm like your freakin' *knight*!' Niki heard him call after her, as she and her friends disappeared along the corridor.

She shrugged at the questioning looks Sangeeta and the others gave her. It still bemused her how someone could go from nearly mugging a person to suddenly being on the same side.

'Short memory, innit,' Chantelle said, when she spoke to her about it.

Idiot, Niki thought zipping up her coat, but she couldn't help smiling when she thought about him later.

♦♦♦♦

Angie knew *something* was going on. For over two weeks now Niki had been different – more closed off, a frown cutting into her forehead.

She'd started asking about her dad, too. It had been a long time since she'd asked questions about him. They'd gone through phases and finally one day Angie had sat her down and said, 'Look, your father loved you, but he was into illegal things and he was violent. A frightening, violent man. So it was for your safety – for both our safety – that we had to leave him behind, OK? He is not in our life for good reason. We're safe now. You have nothing to worry about.'

She'd managed to avoid further questions for a long time, promising to tell Niki more when she was older. . . In time. . . Not yet. . .

And for a while that had satisfied her. She'd

accepted Angie's hugs and her answers of, 'As long as there are the two of us. . . I love you and that's what matters. . . We've got each other. . .'

But then the other night Niki had suddenly asked exactly how long they'd lived with him. What did it matter, she'd asked. Why wasn't she enough?

A new cafe had just opened up opposite the Broadway tube. Angie went in and ordered a skinny latte. With her mug precariously full, she took the stairs gingerly up to the first floor.

Niki had asked for rice and beans the other night.

'Rice and *beans*?' Angie had said. '*Baked* beans?'

'I don't know,' Niki had said, suddenly awkward. 'Whatever beans they eat in Jamaica.'

'I've no idea what beans they eat in Jamaica.'

'Just forget it.'

Later that day Angie's dad had come back from the shops with the *Rough Guide to Jamaica*.

'What on earth are you doing with that?'

'I got it out of the library.'

'What *for*?' she'd asked.

Robert had turned to a page and held it under her nose. Local foods. Rice and beans. Chicken and rice. Jerk chicken. Jerk everything. Ackee and saltfish. Curry goat.

Well, I'm not cooking *goat,* Angie had thought.

'Got this too,' he said plonking an enormous loaf of hard-dough bread on the table with the smug look of a cat placing a dead bird at her feet.

'Mixed Blessings the bakery is called. I have walked past that place for I-don't-know-how-long and never once gone in. It smells marvellous on a Saturday morning – they queue up outside, all along the pavement, waiting for fresh bread. And this is the first time I've ever been in! No idea what to get. I just said, "What's your basic loaf?" and they said, "Hard dough bread." "Doesn't make it sound too appetising," I said and she laughed and laughed. Anyway, so I've no idea what it'll—'

'Why are you *encouraging* her?' interrupted Angie.

He'd looked hurt. He really could pull that mournful look, fix his mouth like a little child, just like Niki did.

'She doesn't *need* encouraging.'

'If she's going to start looking into her heritage then you've got to be prepared. Trust me. It'll be better in the long run than turning a blind eye.'

Wouldn't encouraging Niki to pursue this unknown part of her drive her further on – further away?

What if she turned around and said she wanted to get to know her father?

♠♠♠♠

Angie couldn't tell whether she had ever really loved Damien. She thought yes, albeit a school girl's love – naïve infatuation. At twenty-three he'd seemed like he knew everything. And for a long time she hadn't known what he did to make all his money. He never took the drugs himself. He had simply been cool, and that was all that had mattered.

She remembered at primary school one boy telling her that her dad looked like a librarian. And in a moment she'd realised that there must be something about her dad – the way he'd dressed that morning, or the way he walked, or how he'd said goodbye to her at the school gates. (How old had she been – seven, six?) There was something he had done, which this boy had seen, that had been laughable. She'd always felt there was a point to prove, something to get over – her parents' normality, their dullness. From a very young age, she realised, she'd harboured this desire for admiration, to be in the middle of things, to stand out. And as she'd got older this had developed into a desire to be at the cutting edge, to shock, to be seen as the 'out there' one.

And, of course, a beautiful, black drug dealer had

been the last word in edgy, out-there coolness amongst her friends. Oh yes. She had been *it*.

It had all been wonderful to begin with. Fun. Nothing dangerous or murky or downright evil about the life of a drug dealer. Nothing sordid about what he got up to. Nothing to fear about the choices she made.

And she knew she had given him kudos, too – this tight-bodied teenager sitting in his car. She saw his mates look at her with hungry grins, slapping him on the back, giving knowing little winks.

Angie shook her head, scornful of herself. Seeing those men nodding their approval at Damien, she had felt *pleased* with herself, proud as though this sort of admiration was what she'd been looking for. She'd thought they'd admired *her*, as a person. She gulped at her coffee, awash with humiliation.

When she met Damien, her gymnastics came to an end. Until then she'd messed about a bit – going out with her friends whenever she could – but she had still made her after-school training. She never drank too much on Saturday nights and had always arrived at her Sunday competitions on time, driven silently by her father.

He, she could tell, was too nervous about the

competition, too angry about her staying out, too afraid of her quietness, her distance from him – this girl, this stranger – to ever say a word. She, tired from her partying, equally nervous, was relieved at the quiet. And, increasingly, she felt too far from this silent man, too fed up with him, bored by him, to bother trying to strike up a conversation. It was like he wasn't even there, she'd think.

But in the exhilaration of the competition, their yawning, growing division was often forgotten. They were back to the focused little girl and the heart-in-his-mouth father, both fixed on the prize. Maybe not immediately on arrival. Not as she warmed up and he held her bag, not as she waved an offhand goodbye and went to sit with her coach and team while he found a place in the stands. But as soon as she began. That was the moment when they were united in their very guts. A desperate pulse of love and determination, of grit and sudden fear of loss – loss of the competition but something else too.

Come on, Ange! She could see him willing her with his every blood vessel when she sought him out in the crowd. They would smile and lock eyes, with no remembrance of all that had separated them only an hour or so ago. Those were the moments when they were family again.

But then she started losing. Her focus was gone. She had drunk too much on Saturday nights, she had taken to skipping training after school. She was no longer as good as the girls she competed against, it was as simple as that. And so her eyes didn't seek him out in the crowd because she was too busy looking down at her feet having just fluffed a dismount.

Soon the competitions fizzled out completely.

♦♦♦♦

Angie's coffee had gone cold. She supposed she should go to the shops, seeing as the reason for her little trip – washing up liquid, broccoli, decaf coffee – had yet to be fulfilled.

The problem with Niki reminding her about moving in with Damien, starting to ask increasingly pointed questions, was not only that it brought back memories of how everything had deteriorated into a horrible, frightening mess. The problem was that it also reminded her why they'd moved out of her parents' home, too. She saw Robert pulling out his book on Jamaica, his hard-dough bread, trying to make all this effort, advising her about what to do with her daughter. It highlighted how he'd been the complete opposite when it came to her.

Was he trying to say that, given a second chance, he'd have done things differently? If it happened again would he have got a book on teenage pregnancy out of the library and pulled some Farley's Rusks from his shopping bag? Was it all an elaborate, unspoken apology? It was hard to tell, and if it *was* meant to be that, then it was too backhanded to count. She hated how petulant she sounded, but where had he been all those years ago when she had needed him most? In his study with the door closed, that's where.

It had been an exhausting, frightening initiation into motherhood. Nikita just wouldn't stop crying. Breastfeeding was weird and hurt like hell.

Her health visitor had been a woman named Glory – a broad-shouldered Nigerian woman with hair extensions that were different every time and long nails painted in an assortment of violent colours. Angie broke down often when Glory visited, told her about her mum and dad fighting and the way her dad got annoyed when Nikita cried.

'It's like then he can't pretend she isn't there 'cause she's making so much noise – she's screaming too loud to be invisible.'

'Well, of course she's not invisible.' Glory cooed into Nikita's docile face. 'You're not invisible, are you? No, you're not.'

Often Angie answered the door to Glory with Nikita screaming on her hip, looking as if her head would explode it had gone such a dark red. But Niki always stopped as soon as Glory took hold of her.

'What's all this ruckus, hey? What's all this noise you makin', hmmm? You're gonna drive your mamma *nuts*, girl, you gotta give Mummy a break!'

And she'd put her arm around Angie's shoulder – still in her pyjamas, her skin dull with tiredness, her hair greasy, tied into the same ponytail for a couple of days now.

'You go have a bath and wash that hair of yours and then we'll chat,' Glory would say. 'Leave me to talk to Madam here. Now, you listen to me, Miss High and Mighty. . .'

Sometimes, Angela told Glory, she left Nikita crying upstairs and sat on the sofa in the living room with her head in her hands.

'That's fine,' said Glory. 'That's *good*, trust me.' Then she'd hug Angie again. 'You're doing fine, honestly.'

Angie dreaded her school friends visiting. She hated how they eyed her unbrushed hair and puked-on sweatshirt as though she were covered in boils.

They went wide-eyed when she breastfed, pulling faces that said 'gross!' as plain as day.

As they talked, the stark reality of diverging paths soaked in like rain through cotton. They were getting exam results – getting ready for A-levels, NVQs or had gone straight into jobs.

Her friends were entering the adult world – they could work in offices, dress in pencil skirts and have independence. Whereas she was stuck in her parents' house with tracksuit bottoms and greasy hair. She looked like all those single mums she watched on *Trisha*. How could being pregnant have felt so exciting, daredevil, only to then turn out to be so scary and *exhausting* and, well, conventional? The very thing she'd been seeking her whole life to avoid.

It was fine when Nikita was sleeping.

'She's so cuuuuuute!' and they'd coo over her and hold her like she might suddenly break in their hands.

Angie would give a tired smile then and love her so much. She had never expected to feel such immediate, ferocious, desperate love. She *did* love her, that was definite. She would never give her up, never be without her. Angie would look at her father as he walked through on his way to the kitchen and wonder, is *this* how he feels about *me*?

And where was Damien through all of this? Well, he visited with super-soft toys and Babygros.

When she'd told him she was pregnant he had said, 'Whoa.' Like the Fonz in *Happy Days*, she'd thought. 'Whoa.' It hadn't been the response she'd hoped for. His face didn't break into a grin. He didn't sweep her into his arms and twirl her in the air. He didn't say, 'We're going to be a family!' and start planning when she should move in, like in all those fantasies she'd harboured before finally telling him the news.

No.

He'd said, 'Whoa.'

Like he was trying to slow down a horse that was galloping away with him.

*Whoooaa.*

And then, 'Shit.'

It had never once occurred to her – until that 'Whoa', until that 'Shit' – that this might mean the end of their relationship.

'You're not going to leave me, are you?' she'd found herself saying, suddenly the little girl again, bottom lip trembling.

''Course not. Don't be stupid.' And finally he'd hugged her, but she knew he was looking over her head, off into the distance – as though after that galloping horse that was now careering out of view along with all his freedom.

Their mothers had met – Betsy and Damien's mum, Cheryl. His dad wasn't around.

'Dat's quite cultural,' Angie had heard Hyacinth saying to her mum one afternoon in the back garden. 'Men get de woman pregnant and den up and leave dem to it. Happenin' arl de time. No *stickability*. 'S'why all de kids are runnin' around crazy-wild deez days, uh-mm.'

She didn't hear her mum's reply, but heard Hyacinth quickly adding, 'Oh, *yes*, of *course*. *Damien* gonna stick. He not like *arl* dem other boys. Him different. Him a good boy.'

The mums had agreed that Angie should stay at home until after the baby was born. It was all a big change and she was very young.

Angie wasn't so sure – she wanted to be with Damien, to be a family.

But he'd agreed with the parents. 'Definitely for the best.'

'Just for now?'

'Of course, just for now.'

'Then we'll be together?'

'Right. I said dat.'

And, amazingly, Angie thought, gathering her coat and bag and heading out of the coffee shop, that had been enough to reassure her.

# ELEVEN

That night they ate jerk chicken with rice and peas and fried plantain.

'How's that for a meal?' Angie asked with a weary smile.

Niki nodded her approval and said it was delicious. Perhaps it was all just a sign of puberty at work, Angie thought, relaxing a little, all these ups and downs. Maybe this was further evidence of Niki's transition into womanhood and they would simply have to batten down the hatches and get used to the tumult of period pains and unpredictable mood swings.

She could picture herself in the coming years living for those few glimpsed smiles. Like Brits yanking their clothes off as soon as the sun came out, she would bask in snatches of Niki's good humour – say such things to Robert as, 'Do you remember when she smiled last October?' and they'd laugh.

Robert went into the sitting room to catch the

news, leaving Niki to help her mum clear the kitchen table. Niki picked up a tea towel to start drying the plates and pans.

'Thanks, love.' Angie looked up, her forearms immersed in soapy water.

Niki dried a plate silently, put it into the cupboard, leaving the door open for the rest, then came back to the sink.

'Tell me about my dad,' she said. 'Damien,' she added into the silence.

Damien. The name hung in the air between them, a spider on a thread. It felt strange to say it in front of her mum. This taboo word, this disembodied name. It was hard to believe that the word *Damien* connected to a real person. And harder still to believe that the person attached to that name was in turn attached to her, deeply, by blood.

♠♠♠♠

Angie sighed. So cooking Jamaican food wasn't going to be enough. What should she tell her? How much fun he'd been when they first met – how they'd raced around in that stupid car of his, how they'd made love on his sitting room floor and he'd laughed at her getting drunk on her vodka and orange juices. How he could lift her off the ground with a single arm.

How when he found out she was having his baby he'd said, 'Whoa. . . Shit.'

How he'd visited, but she could see the sense of duty of it, see him slipping away. And she had to leave message after message on his phone before he called her back.

Would she tell Niki about when they finally moved in to Damien's? How she'd nagged and pressured until he'd finally said, 'All *right*.' And she knew she'd won, but there was no joy in it, just a sense of misery, of sand trickling through her fingers, but now she had to follow through because she'd pinned everything on this fact – that Damien still wanted her. That they belonged together.

She would show her father that she wasn't a complete screw up. They would manage, and not only manage, but do well – be a proper family. Go to the parks together like she saw other people do when she wheeled Niki up there with her mum or on her own. There she saw dads aeroplaning children over their heads, waiting for them at the bottom of slides, walking home with babies strapped into buggies and arms around the mums. That would be them.

'You can come back anytime you need to,' Betsy had said.

'Mum!'

'Look, I'm just saying. You're always welcome. You're only five minutes away so call *whenever* you need to, OK? There's always a place for you here.'

If I was asked, Angie thought, to sketch my life over that next period, I would draw a plane falling out of the sky.

Niki's sleeping patterns were thrown by moving into their new home, not helped by the fact that the traffic was noisier and the neighbours stayed up late watching television.

Each breath Niki took when she cried was so deep that Angie could see the muscles under her skin heave with exertion, could see her body flex right down to those impossibly tiny toes. Angie would hold her out at arms length, her hands clutched around this torso – inside of which she could feel every heartbeat hammering away at what seemed like unhealthy speed – Niki cycling her legs, pushing against the air with every scream. Angie would hold her there and feel Niki's entire ribcage expand as she filled her lungs. She would watch Niki's face crumple, her skin turn to the colour of a plum, her mouth open so wide Angie felt consumed by it.

And somewhere in amongst it all, this intense loneliness, Angie began to face up to the fact that Damien did not love her, did not want them in his house, in his life, as his responsibility. . . But although her mum had said she could call, how *could* she call – in the middle of the night, crying, whispering into the phone, asking what she should do as Niki kept on screaming and the people downstairs turned up the volume of their TV in retaliation.

She couldn't bear the thought of arriving home and having to face an *I told you so* look from her dad.

So she sat in Damien's house day and night, never quite knowing where he was or when he would be coming home. Not answering the phone because she knew she'd cry at the sound of a friend's voice, not daring to venture to the mums and tots groups because they'd see how she wasn't coping.

In amongst all of this she began to realise that the changes in Damien were more complicated than she had suspected.

She felt his resentment changing, darkening, beginning to scare her. She could see it in his eyes and clenched jaw.

She finally realised that, for some time now, Damien must have gone from dealing drugs to taking them.

And the first time she confronted him was the moment her lonely, self-pitying misery turned to outright terror.

That was the first time she had to hide her baby under the bed. . .

♠♠♠♠

'Come *on*, Mum, you said you would.'

'No, I'm sorry, I can't. I can't do it.' Throwing the dishcloth into the sink, Angie ran up to her bedroom and hid her face in her pillow.

♠♠♠♠

'I t'ought you were never comin' back ta see me.'

'I had some thinking to do.'

Hyacinth stepped back to let Niki in.

'Well, you come wid me.'

She led Niki upstairs and into a bedroom that was obviously intended for guests, but never used. The bed was laid with a crocheted blanket over the top of its neatly-tucked sheets. On the pillow was some sort of flannel, it seemed to Niki, with a posy of dried rosebuds, dulled to a tea-stained brown. Pages torn from magazines had been framed and hung on the wall – sandy beaches and turquoise seas, a couple walking into a sunset, a map of Jamaica with a Thomson Holidays logo in the corner.

'In dat cupboard are me Christmas decorations. Get 'um for me, dere's a dear.'

Niki pulled out the box and brushed off some dust with her hand.

'Can you believe it's gonna be December tomorrow – hey? Christmas! I *love* Christmas, when we celebrate de dear Lord Jesus comin' into de world. It a good time, nah.'

'A family time,' Niki said quietly.

'Dear girl, you got a family! A family dat *love* you.'

'I *know*.' Niki let out a sigh, her whole torso sagging into it. 'It's not that. Why is everyone making it so hard? Surely it's *normal* to want to know about my dad?'

'Carry de box downstairs and I make us somet'ing to drink.'

Niki sat on the sitting room floor untangling coloured fairy lights from balding strings of tinsel. Next to her was a mug of watery hot chocolate with granules still floating around on the top, but no spoon to stir them.

'I just want to know about him,' she said, interrupting Hyacinth's story about her son taking his family back to Jamaica for Christmas, so her being a little unsure as to what she'd be doing for Christmas herself.

Hyacinth sucked her teeth and raised her chin. 'So. An' have you asked your mammy 'bout dis?'

'I *tried*! But she wouldn't talk to me. Look. OK. I get that you don't want to cause upset. But I know about him now, so there's no use pretending I don't. He's around – and he's OK. Like, an OK person. And so I think that it's . . . it's my *right* to know about him.'

'Arl right, I'm gettin' de message.' She muttered under her breath, sucked her teeth again and then asked, 'So, what you wanna know? He been married for 'bout five years now and he ha' two little girls. . .'

'Well, where he lives, I guess.'

'Where he *lives*? But what you gonna do? You can't go seein' 'im. No, dear me, no. You said you want to know *about* 'im, nat see 'im. Dat two *very* different t'ings.'

'Yeah, well, it's going to lead to seeing him, isn't it? I mean, even if just once. *Just once*. He's my dad!'

This time the sucking breath through Hyacinth's teeth seemed to go on for an impossibly long time. She stuck her false teeth forwards over her bottom lip and her little eyes stretched as round as they could go. She shook her head slowly from side to side, her whole face in spasm with anxiety.

'I don't know about dis. You need to be talkin' to your mammy.'

'But she doesn't want to know. And, look, OK, if you tell me where he lives, I can just go see it – see *him*. And then that'll be it. It's just to know. And this way we won't hurt Mum.'

'I t'ink you is bitin' off more dan you can be chewin'.'

'It's OK, really, I've thought about it. I just want to go and see where he lives.' She tried to make it sound so simple, so small, holding up her palm as though asking for a penny. 'See him *just once*. That's enough. I love my mum. I have my family now with Grandad. It's not to change things or make her feel bad or anything. It's just to *know*. 'Cause all I know about him – all I *think* I know – well, I think it's all wrong. 'Cause, like, you've told me that he's a good person and. . .' She didn't know how to explain the fear that had hung over her for as long as she could remember. The phantom stalker who crept into her room, climbed through the window of her dreams.

Maybe, if she could go – just once – and see him, see a normal man, all of that *stuff* would just disappear. Then she – she *and* her mum – wouldn't have to be afraid.

She could never leave things as they were now, knowing so much and yet practically nothing, knowing that everything she had thought until now could be wrong.

And yet how could she be sure that this new version of the story was true? A good, ordinary man? How could a person change in the space of a conversation? A few words from a neighbour telling her that he was a good person, that his prison sentence had been more of a misunderstanding, that he wasn't bad really. She had to know for herself.

It was a moment of growing up – she could sense it – thinking this through all on her own. She had an awareness of all her bones, of anticipation tingling around the edges of an emptiness inside her – a hole waiting to be filled with knowledge that was soon to be hers. The finding out of it, seeking it independently. It gave her a Christmas Eve kind of thrill. She felt taller, thinner, less childish, sitting cross-legged on Hyacinth's floor, polishing red and gold baubles in the pleats of her skirt.

Hyacinth watched her for a while, but Niki pretended not to notice. She tried to engross herself in shining the baubles until her warped reflection could be seen bulging towards her with a curving, witchy nose. She knew to bide her time, to not whine, to wait. She wouldn't give Hyacinth anything to pull against. Just let the idea, the – what was the word? – the *unstoppability* of it, hang loosely, lightly, in such a way that couldn't be resisted.

Inside she was thinking, come on. Come *onnnn*. But she kept on gently rolling the baubles over her skirt, waiting.

'Oh, I don't know.'

'Thank you, thank you. You won't regret it, honest. Thank you, Hyacinth.'

'I really ain't sure we be doin' dis right.'

'It's the best way, it really is.'

'I get me address book,' she heaved herself out of the low armchair. She was wearing fingerless gloves and kept tucking her hands underneath her armpits.

'So we gotta phone 'is mamma for 'is address, but what we gonna say? How do I arks for 'is address when I don't never make contact wid 'im before? It seem too strange, nah.'

'Just say . . . say you want to send a Christmas card, or you want to ask about the nursery his girls go to for someone's child, or something.'

Hyacinth looked up, her glasses pulled down to the very tip of her nose because she found it easier to read over the top of them. 'You seem a bit good at *lyin'*.'

'I'm only trying to help.'

'Hmm.' She pursed her lips, then held her address book close to her eyes. 'Here it is, den. I carl her up. Yes. I'll gi' her a carl.'

Eventually, Hyacinth stopped studying the address book and met Niki's gaze.

'What you lookin' at me like dat for?'

'Well . . . there's no time like the present.'

'Oh my days. You is as stubborn and as fixed as dat old goat you call a grandaddy. Dear me, chil', give me a moment to be gadderin' me resources.' With a deep breath, she heaved herself back out of her chair and walked through to the kitchen to where she kept her phone.

Niki followed and stood in the doorway. When Hyacinth saw her there she turned her back, put the address book on the worktop and dialled.

'Hello? Yes, I am carlin' Cheryl, she dere? Cheryl! It Hyacinth Johnson! Yes! Yes! Fine. Fine. And how are you? Yes. I know, it bin dat long, I am sorry for it.'

They talked on while Niki tapped her fingers against the doorframe, biting her bottom lip.

'An' your boy, how he doin' now? Oh, dat good. Oh, yes, very good. . . I were just wonderin' 'is address. . .' She turned in a fluster, mouthing *Pen! Pen!* and writing in the air. Niki darted into the other room and found a pen, bringing it with an envelope for Hyacinth to write on.

'So dat's number two Lansdowne Road. Mm-hmm. Well t'ank you, Cheryl. We need to be meetin' up soon. Christmas, oh yes, I got big plans, yes, t'ank you. OK. OK. . . OK. . . Bye now. . .' It seemed to take forever to hang up the phone. Hyacinth leant closer and closer to it, holding the receiver further and further away from her ear. 'Bye now.' And then the receiver was crashed down. She let out a deep breath.

'Oh my! 'Ere it is! And she didn't even arks me why I be needin' it, she just give it me, just like dat! Oh my!'

They hugged each other as Niki thanked her again. She looked down at the spidery writing. Her dad had an address. A home.

♦♦♦♦

That night Niki folded up the envelope into neat squares. She thought about putting it under her pillow, but knew that the amount she rolled around in her sleep might mean it ended up lying in the open when her mum came to wake her in the morning.

She had constantly imagined this mystery figure lurking under her bed, and now, as she slid the envelope between the bed frame and her mattress, she felt that he somehow was.

# TWELVE

'You want de two-six-four to Croydon,' Hyacinth told her. 'Get off at Tamworth Road. 'Ere. Den it's de other side of de shoppin' centre. See?' she said pointing in her A to Z. 'Take it wid you.'

⁂

On the bus Niki watched a man holding onto a rail above his head. His belly was big enough for triplets, hanging over his trousers. She watched him scratch inside his ear with the ring finger of his free hand, transferring whatever he found onto his thumb, looking at it and then eating it. Niki looked away. Another man sat doing a crossword, concentrating with the tip of his tongue clamped between his lips. She counted seven sets of iPod headphones.

Beside her, Chantelle chattered non-stop.

'I've worked out what I'm gonna get, yeah. So,

right, I wan' *white* dungarees, right, really baggy and I'll 'ave 'em like half down, you know, the straps hangin' down, and den wiv a vest top I guess. . . I've still got birfday money left over – I was fifteen de first week o' school. September de ninf. Oldest in our form. Anywayz, so I've brought de lot. Time I used it up. When's your birfday, anyway?'

'First of July.'

'Oh my *days*, you is a *baby*!'

When Chantelle asked her what she was doing on the weekend, Niki had mumbled something about not having been to Croydon. It was the talk of all the girls' weekends – who'd gone to the Croydon shopping centre, what they'd bought.

'Oh, *yeah*, man, I'm in,' Chantelle said before Niki had a chance to realise she should have been more vague.

In a way she was pleased to have company for the bus journey going to a place she'd never been before. And it had made it easier to get permission from her mum. Chantelle had come to her house so Angie could give them both the ground rules about when to be back, about not going anywhere other than the shopping centre, making sure they had credit on their phones. . .

'Bit strict, your mum, ain't she?'

'Gross!' said Chantelle, when she noticed the man eating the deposits from his ear. He glanced up, and then looked out of the window, wiping his hands on his trousers.

'Did you see dat?!' She nudged Niki. 'Dirty *dog*.'

'Shut up, he can hear you.'

'Well, I *mean*!' She offered Niki a sour worm sweet. 'So, anyway, whatchu gonna get?'

'I don't know, really. I might just do some Christmas shopping.'

'Yeah, it ain't long now – I can't *wait*! My bruvver is gettin' a Nintendo Wii – can you believe it? I reckon I'll get . . . I don't know, I haven't decided. . . I just had loads of money for clothes so I'm finkin' maybe a new phone. . . Dat's what I love about Christmas and birfdays – you can just get what you *want*, like, money ain't no object.'

Christmas had never been like that for Niki but she nodded anyway. She wondered why, if Chantelle's mum could afford to buy them whatever they wanted, they lived in a house with not enough bedrooms.

She was beginning to feel nervous. Maybe today she'd just go to the shopping centre – get to know the bus route and leave it at that. Maybe buy dungarees, too, and then come back another time to actually find her dad's house. She sucked her jelly sweet and tried to keep up with what Chantelle was talking about.

'You're in a world of yer own today, innit.'

'Sorry. I'm just – I don't know. . .'

'Eat anuvver of deez. Sugar rush. It'll send ya hyper in no time.'

Nearly everyone got off at the same stop and headed towards the shopping centre that stood over them – all glass and sharp corners – like a giant iceberg.

It was gone two o'clock – everywhere was busy with Saturday shoppers. She found herself having to hunch her shoulders to squeeze through narrow spaces.

How could she do this, anyway? She could hardly just slip away without Chantelle knowing. Maybe she could suggest they split up and meet in half an hour, but that might seem weird. Besides, she wasn't sure how long it would take her to find this road, anyway. She wasn't very good with maps. She had looked and looked at the page in the A to Z, tracing the route, but now she was here she wasn't quite sure which direction she'd be heading in – which corner of the shopping centre she needed to *start* from.

Chantelle was skipping along beside her, clapping her hands.

'*And* what we need to do is buy *you* some elastics, den we can do your hair again – sort out dat *frizz* dat's comin' back, man!'

As soon as they were through the automatic doors, which were held open constantly because of the steady stream of people going in and out, Chantelle grabbed Niki's arm and pulled her towards the first clothes shop.

'OK. De hunt is on.'

She started grabbing things off the rails, holding them up to herself, discarding them, fingering things on the jewellery stand, posing in front of the mirror.

'What abou' dis. . .? Ooh, what d'you fink of *dis*?' she kept asking Niki, who would nod and say, 'Yeah, really nice.' And it was true – everything seemed made for Chantelle's energetic, leggy body. Her tiny waist and already obvious breasts.

'Ain't you gonna try anyfing on?' Chantelle asked.

Niki looked around. She had no idea what she wanted. She felt stuck between two things that she didn't want. She didn't want to be shopping and holding up clothes. But she wasn't sure she could bring herself to go and find this road.

'Take dis an' dis an' dis, right, an' follow me.'

Niki's arms were suddenly laden with clothes. She followed Chantelle into the changing rooms.

'Show me everyfing, yeah. We're gonna give you a makeover! Den you'll *never* be able to get Tyrone off yer back!' She cackled and thumped Niki's arm, then swished the curtain closed so that Niki was left standing in front of her reflection.

She stared at herself for a long time. She couldn't see any of her mother in her.

♠♠♠♠

Sitting in McDonalds with McFlurries and chips, Chantelle leant back in her seat.

'So, are you gonna tell me or wot?'

'What?'

'Summink's up. You're bein' all weird. You've bin, like, quiet as the grave.'

Niki shrugged.

'Come on, neeky girl, we've bought you a nice little skirt and some nice little tops. You should be buzzin'.' Chantelle sucked the ice cream off her plastic spoon. 'If you don't tell me what's wrong, I'll phone Tyrone right now and tell 'im you like 'im.'

Niki smiled in spite of herself.

'Come on, you know you want to.'

Niki chewed her top lip and mixed up her ice cream, watching it melt as she mushed it around.

'You mustn't tell anyone.'

'Cross my heart,' said Chantelle in an accent that mimicked Niki's. She drew an X just under her left collarbone. 'Oh, come *on*, you're killin' me.'

'Well. So. I've found out, OK . . . that . . . my dad . . . isn't in prison. . .'

Chantelle leant forward, her mouth open, a drop of ice cream falling from her spoon onto the table.

'So, where is 'e, den?'

'In Croydon.'

'You're messin'.'

Niki shook her head.

'. . . An' you're here to find 'im.'

'I've got his address and,' she pulled out the A to Z, 'he lives right here. Number two.'

'*Is it?!* Wow, Nik, you found 'im? Oh my days. . . So,' she changed into her best Jamaican, 'what de bloody 'ell are we doin' sittin' 'ere in Maccy D's den?' She leant back in her seat and reached for her bag with a questioning look. 'Are we goin' or wot?'

Here was Niki's choice. She'd got his address, she

wanted to know more, she knew she did. But there would be no going back. As yet he was barely any more real to her than he had ever been. Whether he was in prison or Croydon – or Outer Mongolia – he still wasn't in her life. He remained kind of like a character from telly or out of a book and maybe she could just slowly adapt her story over time. Maybe that was enough. She wouldn't fear him and he would morph into a distant, gentle figure whom she could reinvent in various ways as and when she liked.

By going to the house, seeing a real, solid house – everything would become real.

She looked at Chantelle who was still waiting, the same questioning stare in her eyes. With a nod from Niki, they grabbed their bags and left.

'So, which way?'

Niki looked at the page. 'We're looking for Lansdowne. Right here,' she pointed.

'OK, so we need to get out dis side, over Wellesley, up Syd-ham, or wha'ever it's called – aaand . . . turn into Bedford, dere. Den dat's it. OK?' She shook Niki's arm. 'Come on, Nik, you're doin' de right fing. It's brave, girl.'

Niki gave an anxious grin. 'Let's go.'

⁂⁂

They stood on the corner of the road, looking across at number two. There it was. A semi-detached, red-brick house with a blue front door.

'Nice,' Chantelle said.

Niki chewed her lip and felt the urge to cry.

'You OK?' Chantelle asked.

Niki nodded but didn't dare speak. They stood side by side for a while.

'So, what'll you do, den?' Chantelle asked after a bit, stamping her feet to warm up.

Niki could feel herself getting cold as well, as though all the warmth from her body had just soaked out of her into the air. It was a bone-aching chill that stiffened her fingers and bit into her cheeks. Lights were being turned on in the houses around them.

'Well, they're obviously not in,' she said.

'You ain't gonna, I dunno, leave a note or summink?'

'No. I mean, his wife might not know about me for a start. Can you imagine? If I do anything, it'll have to be in person. But not yet – I just wanted to see the place, you know? It's really real.' A family lived inside it. *He* lived inside it.

A red car pulled up and parked outside, causing

Niki and Chantelle to step back instinctively as a man and woman got out.

Tall, much darker than herself, darker than Chantelle, even – was this him? His hair was very short. He wore a smart three-quarter length coat and black trousers. It looked like they were all back from a party because Niki could see that the woman was wearing high-heeled shoes and elaborate, dangling earrings. Niki's heart pounded, pounded, pounded.

The adults opened up the back doors of the car on either side and unstrapped two children, each lifting one onto their hips, two girls in dresses, brightly coloured coats, thick tights and identical pink boots. The man went to the boot and took out some bags with his other hand, managing to close the boot and lock the car with both arms full. The little girl snuggled into his shoulder, her arms clinging around his neck. He and the woman were talking to each other and Niki saw his face break into a smile as he kissed the top of the sleeping girl's head.

They walked up to the front door of number two. He put down the bags to unlock the door and waited for the woman to go in ahead of him, then followed her inside, closing the door with his foot.

'No *way,*' whispered Chantelle.

'It's time we left,' Niki said and bolted as fast as she could, hearing Chantelle calling behind her, *'Wait for meeee!'* But she didn't slow down.

♠♠♠♠

I'll give you one more chance, Niki thought, looking at her.

'Tell me about my dad,' she said.

'Oh, Nik.' Angie felt exhausted by these questions. *Why* did she need to know about him? What was so worth hearing about?

'OK,' she said, wearily.

Niki leant back in her seat, ready to listen.

'I was fifteen. I got pregnant – had you at sixteen. We lived here and it was a disaster. We moved in with him and it was worse—'

'How worse?'

'He was horrible, OK? I'm sorry to say it, but he was frightening and abusive and I *don't want to talk about it*!'

'And he's in prison.'

*'Yes!'*

'But that was after we'd left.'

'Your grandma called and told me that he was put

away. It wasn't for what he did to us, it was for other stuff. But by then we were doing our own thing. I didn't want to move back. Besides there was all this history,' she lowered her voice to say this, indicating with her eyes that Robert was right next door. '*Why* are you doing this? So, we're in Tooting. *So what?* Loads of people don't know one or other of their parents. It's not as though I'm trying to keep some lovely man from you out of jealousy, OK? All of this has been for your own good, do you see? Why can't we just leave it at that?'

Because you're lying, Niki thought. Because he is not in prison. He has a wife and a family, little girls who snuggle into his shoulder. Why would they do that if he was so horrible? And because you said Grandad didn't want me to be born but he's been nice all the time we've been here. He's normal. He eats cake and watches *Countdown*.

Because there's a half of me that's missing.

*And* you lied about Granny Smith. Now she's dead and it's too late. But it's not too late with my dad.

♦♦♦♦

On the night before the last day of term, Niki went

round to Chantelle's to get her braids redone.

As usual there were toys, a PlayStation Portable, scooters, dolls, remote-controlled cars scattered everywhere – in the hallway, on the sofas, on the kitchen table. Computer games and DVDs lay spread out across the living room floor, cases open and the discs lying upturned where they'd been discarded.

'Bi' of a mess,' Chantelle said, without sounding embarrassed.

'Hiya,' said Chantelle's mum, Chantez. 'Make yourself at 'ome. Now, Chantelle, you sure you know what you're doin'?'

'*Yes*, Mum, I've done it like a *thousand* million *times*.'

'I was only checkin'. Call me if 'er 'air starts fallin' out. I'm just kiddin'!' she added to Niki.

Niki sat on the toilet in the bathroom while Chantelle massaged oil into her hair. 'Makes it easier to handle.'

'Prepare to be amazed,' she said, grinning and rubbing her hands together.

She worked the oil into Niki's hair with fast, nimble fingers.

'Me and mum do each uvver's all de time.'

She had laid out a silky scarf for Niki to borrow that she'd need to wear at night 'to stop breakages'.

'Do you mind your dad not being around much?' Niki asked, trying to keep her head still.

''S'orite. I mean, he is around, really. Like, Tyrone's dad, well, Ty don't even know him at all. So, different people have different situations, don' dey? It's not like everyone else has dis happy life. Everyone's got summink they'd change, given half the chance. You just deal wiv what you've got, don't you?'

'I guess.'

'Like, I've been finking about you. I mean, if you get to know your dad – well, what do you imagine is going to be so different? I used to fink, if only my dad were OK, lived at home, had a job – was like uvver dads. But den you got Tyrone finkin', if only I *knew* my dad, full stop. And you've got your mate Sangeeta finkin', if only my dad could get a *decent* job. Den she'd actually get to see 'im.'

Niki had talked about Sangeeta to Chantelle and they were starting to say hi to each other in the school corridors.

'And den,' Chantelle continued, 'dere'll be some poor kid finkin, if only my dad would piss off out of my life – 'cause he's beatin' the crap out of dem, or summink. You know? No one has the perfect life. No dad's gonna bring all de magic answers.'

'I know that.'

'Just so long as you do.'

It took three hours to do Niki's hair.

'Cool, huh?' grinned Chantelle. 'It makes you look so much older.'

Niki fingered her plaits. They were more elaborate than her previous style and she looked sleeker, stronger. 'Thanks, I love it,' she said quietly, smiling at Chantelle via their reflections.

'I didn't mean to be all down on you earlier. It's just. . . Niki . . . he might not even want to know you. You gotta be prepared – men'ally, like – for a big fat disappointment. Just in case.'

♠♠♠♠

The last day of term was a half day and they were allowed to wear their own clothes. Niki wore her new short skirt, black patterned tights, embroidered ballet pumps that she'd bought at Tooting Market for three pounds and a fitted jumper.

'Wow, look at you,' said Angie. 'My little girl turning into quite the young lady.'

Niki smiled. She was proper Tooting now.

# THIRTEEN

The sky was a steel grey, streaked with grubby clouds. Now that she was on holiday, Niki could go to Croydon anytime of day she wanted. She bought Christmas presents – a bowl of Bristol glass and five floating candles for her mum; vanilla fudge and a gardening book for Grandad; rose-scented hand cream for Hyacinth. She'd chosen with barely a thought, picking up the first thing that she hoped would do, selecting alibis rather than gifts. Now, once again, she stood outside his house. Today she was going to knock.

At least, she really had intended to. But she had hesitated in her usual place on the pavement, and now that she had stopped the cold had soaked into her and all her determination seemed to have been diluted into chilly indecision. She could see the two girls jumping up and down in the sitting room whilst watching something on the television, then she saw the woman come in and start clapping in time to their leaps. There was no red car.

She left hurriedly, feeling exposed in her short skirt, embarrassed by the boys who whistled at her near the bus stop and shouted out, '*Oi!* Come 'ere! Oh, come on, we just wanna talk!' – laughing to each other and calling, 'I can see your knickers!'

She knew it wasn't true but still she tugged at her skirt, setting off fresh shouts of laughter. 'Dat's right, you sket!'

At home she put the presents under her bed and pulled out a shoebox of photographs that she'd found when clearing space amongst her grandmother's things to make room for her own. They were pictures of her mum mainly from childhood and early teens. As she got older the photos petered out. There was one where she must have been about fourteen – a streak of yellow ran across one corner where the sun had caught the lens at the wrong angle. Angela stood with her weight more on one stick-thin leg than the other, wearing a short denim skirt and black and white chequered plimsolls. Her hair was scraped into a high, wispy ponytail and shimmery lipstick bleached her unsmiling mouth.

Most of the pictures in the shoebox showed Angela when she was a toddler, running around the garden in a swimming costume, or proudly holding up a melting ice cream on a beach, her childish tummy as swollen as a balloon, her skin milky white and hair so blonde she looked albino.

Further on, Niki found another photo of Angela around Niki's age, perhaps a bit younger, wearing a halter neck bikini whilst practising her gymnastics in the back garden. She was leaping in the air, her back foot kicking up behind her, almost touching her head, which was thrown back so that her throat was exposed to the sky. Her toes were pointed so hard that they curled round like cupped hands – her arms flung back impossibly far. Niki hadn't known her mum was a gymnast. She looked incredible – leaping with grace and ease, and yet Niki could see every muscle used, could count every rib. The face in the photo was so her mum's, but somehow completely different, with an enormous sun-burst of a smile. Strands of her hair whipped out around her, waiting for gravity to catch up. Niki looked at the photo for a long time, holding it closer to her face to try and really *see* it. This person, before she was her mother.

It was like with her teachers at school, Niki thought, putting the photo down on the floor next to her. She never imagined teachers as having lives outside the classroom. As if at the end of the school day they simply ceased – like some sort of android that got turned off, head down, arms stiff, waiting at the front of the class until the caretaker came round the next morning and flicked on a switch located at the nape of their necks. Niki realised that she never wondered about whether her teachers had husbands or hobbies, never imagined that perhaps at the end of the school day they might try to fit in a quick swim before meeting friends and going to the cinema.

And here her mother leapt in the air, was someone she didn't know.

No more putting it off, Niki decided. She had to find out who she was. She had to meet her dad.

♠♠♠♠

This time she didn't hesitate. She walked straight over and rang the doorbell. She watched the door open in front of her as though it were happening far, far away, feeling like she had suddenly gone down a dip in a road and left her stomach hanging in the air somewhere behind her. There stood the woman. Her hair was cut close, highlighting a face with delicate bones. She inclined her head to look down at Niki, the rest of her body staying as straight as could be, elegant and quiet, one hand still on the door latch.

They looked at each other, then the woman looked over her shoulder.

'Damien, honey!'

No reply.

*'Damien!'*

'What?' A man's voice came from the front room – Niki could hear him through the window to her left as well as down the hallway.

'Come here please!'

'What?'

His voice sounded closer, but Niki couldn't see him because he was hidden behind the woman's back. She had turned round to look at him.

'What is it?'

'Your past come knocking.'

'What? Oh.'

Niki saw his head over the woman's shoulder. She had laid a hand on his arm and he in turn rested his hand on her waist.

'Oh,' he said again.

'I'll take the girls for their bath, it's nearly time anyway.'

She turned back to Niki.

'Come in, Nikita,' she said.

Niki stepped inside as the woman walked away from her.

'Suki! May! Bathtime!'

The two girls dragged themselves along the hallway with reluctant feet and sulky faces. Niki stood on the front doormat, hands by her sides. Stairs stretched up in front of her on the right. Damien stood with his back against the wall. His arm brushed hers, causing him to take a startled step away as though he'd just been given an electric shock.

'Come on, girls,' he said waving them past, trying to make it seem as though he had really moved to help with the shepherding process.

The older child put her hands on the banister and turned to look at him. 'Do we *have* to have our baths *now*?' she said, narrowing her eyes. 'It's nearly *finished*.'

'You can watch the rest tomorrow,' their mum said, clapping her hands. 'Chop, chop.'

'Who's that?' the other girl asked, her hand pulling on her mum's sweatshirt as she trailed behind her.

'Someone to see your father, May-may, don't *fuss* about it. Come *on* – *scoot*, the both of you!' She herded the second child round in front of her and gave her a gentle push. As she walked past, the little girl kept her eyes fixed on Niki. Niki smiled at her but the girl's expression remained unreadable.

'*Now!*' And in an instant the children were thundering up the stairs, shrieking ecstatically as their mother chased behind, her arms outstretched, hands snapping like pincers.

Niki could hear them giggling, hear the woman saying, 'Clothes off. Who's going to be first?' as the water began to run.

'Sooo . . . Nikita.' He turned to look at her properly for the first time.

Niki saw that their eyes were the same and wondered whether he could see it too.

'Drink? Juice or something?'

She nodded and followed him into the kitchen.

'We've been waiting for this day. I mean, waiting and not waiting. Wondering if you'd ever come,' he said, talking to her over his shoulder as he bent into the fridge.

She wanted to say, 'You could have come looking for me,' but kept quiet, chewing her lower lip.

'We've got Coke if you'd like,' he said, glancing over the fridge door. She nodded.

'Oh, here, let me take your coat. We can go sit down

in the other room.' He handed her the can and took her coat in return. 'Are you happy with it like that or d'you want a glass?'

'This is fine, thanks.'

She followed him into the sitting room. Plastic boxes in primary colours lined one wall, overflowing with toys. Damien picked up stray objects as he made his way into the room, throwing them into the boxes. A Snow White dress that Niki recognised from the Disney cartoon lay crumpled on the floor, along with some bent fairy wings and a wand.

'So. . .' he said, gesturing to an armchair.

Niki sat down on the edge of the chair, pulling her sleeves over her hands to hold the cold can.

'What was I saying? Yes. Waiting – and now I have no idea what to say!'

He looks younger than Mum, Niki thought. Isn't he meant to be older?

His face was smooth – buttery rich skin like her own, only darker, as she'd noticed the first time she'd seen him. He had broad, lean shoulders, and wore a baggy sweatshirt and black tracksuit bottoms with three white stripes running down the sides, the sort of clothes Tyrone and the others wore when they were out of school. On his feet were sports socks – one of them was loose over his toes, slipping off. On his left hand she noticed a gold wedding band and felt a hardness inside her at the sight of it.

'So,' he repeated, smiling awkwardly. 'Well. . . Why *now*? That's not meant, like, to sound unfriendly or anything,' he added hastily. 'I guess I just wonder – yeah, why now? After all this time, you appear on our doorstep tonight.'

'I only found out where you were about three weeks ago. I thought you were in prison.'

His head jerked in surprise, 'What?'

'I only heard that you weren't in prison three weeks ago. Then I found your address and then I came. Well, I've been a few times, just looking, but today I knocked.'

'Right. I'm sorry – you thought I was still in *prison*? I've been out – what? – ten *years* or something!' He looked out of the window, shaking his head and giving a little disbelieving laugh.

'My mum didn't know, if that's what you're thinking,' Niki said, suddenly defensive of her. 'We moved away and no one told us.'

'Harpenden.'

'Then other places.'

'So, how did you hear about me now?'

'We're back in Tooting. My grandad's ill.'

'Oh, yeah. Mr Smith.'

He said his name in the way Niki would speak of her worst teacher.

'And he's ill?'

'He's got cancer. We've come to look after him – my mum's a carer.'

'Well. I'm sorry to hear it. And how's Betsy – your grandma?'

'She died. Four years ago.'

'Oh. I'm sorry. Really. She was a wonderful lady. I'm really sorry.'

Niki could see thoughts racing through his mind, passing over his face like the shadows of clouds.

'She was good to us, to me. . . And you must be fourteen, right? Amazing. It's been a long time. And look at you now. . .' He smiled.

Niki tried to smile back but couldn't quite manage it.

'So was it your grandad who knew where I was, then? *Couldn't* be.'

'No. I don't know what he knows about you. But there's a lady who lives next door to him—'

'Hyacinth? Man, I ain't seen her for I-don't-know-how-long. Well, since around then. Hyacinth! Well,

I never. She knew everything, that woman. . . So she just came out an' told you? I was in prison and then suddenly I wasn't? That must have been quite a shock.'

'Shock doesn't even come close,' Niki replied. 'I came with my friend Chantelle, and we saw you, actually, you were all getting out of your car. . . All my life I've thought you were like—' she hesitated, 'I thought you were a murderer or something.'

'Is that right?'

'Well, you know, prison for years and years – my whole life nearly – I figured you must have done something *really bad*. And . . . other stuff.' She decided suddenly that she didn't want to tell him about her mum's refusal to talk about him, the way she got upset like she had some awful secret to hide or memory too hateful to remember, the way she had kept moving them on as though haunted by his ghost – running, running.

Damien gave a big sigh and stroked the arm of the settee he was sitting on. 'Well. That's a lot to take in. Boy. . .'

There was a knock at the door.

'*Sorry* to interrupt. The girls would like to say goodnight if you don't mind.' The two girls walked into the room in matching candy-hooped pyjamas. Niki noticed their hair this time – both had theirs plaited the same way – slender stalks that sprouted all over their heads, each tightly wrapped with black thread.

'Good night, my girls,' Damien hugged one in each arm, as they kissed him on the lips in turn.

'Good night.' The older girl waved to Niki as she walked past and then the smaller one waved too.

'Sleep tight,' Damien called after them.

'I'll join you soon,' said their mum quietly to Damien.

'Dilani and I have been married for nearly seven years now,' he said once they'd gone. 'Suki has just turned five and May is three.'

Niki noticed that all the photos in the room were of the family – portraits of the children, Damien and Dilani's wedding day, the whole family sitting on a beach together, a girl in the lap of each parent. Niki wondered who had taken the picture.

'Dilani and I have talked about what we'd do if you turned up one day. And the first thing I want you to know is that I'm glad you're here. I'm glad to know you.'

'What did you do?'

'I'm sorry?'

'Why were you in prison?'

'Oh. OK. Right. Yeah, well, you see. . . I was in a very bad place around the time I knew Ange. Basically . . . I dealt drugs – and, well, I got *into* drugs. And someone *did* die – it wasn't murder. It was a road accident. I was on drugs at the time and I killed someone, a young man. Nineteen years old. I killed him. I was given seven years.

'Amazingly – and I know this might sound odd – but prison was the best thing that ever could have happened to me. I don't think many people who end up inside would say that – lots of them just get dragged down and down and down, you know. But for me it was the wake-up call I needed. I got clean and I vowed that once I got out I would stay clean. I was out after four years on good behaviour. Nothing I can do will ever make up for what I did to that man and his family.'

What about me and my family? Niki wondered.

'And you didn't stay in touch with Mum.'

'She left with you before that stuff happened. I was in a bad way, like I said. It was right that she left. I was getting worse and worse, and then this happened. Total rock bottom, end of the line stuff. It was good that you weren't there.

'So, you see, it wasn't possible to be looking for her at the time, you know? And, frankly, why would she have wanted me to? Well, and then four years had gone by. . .'

'So then, you didn't try—'

'No, I suppose I didn't try.'

Niki watched his whole chest rise and fall with one big breath.

'But it wasn't quite like that, OK?' he added.

The door opened again. Dilani came and sat on the couch next to Damien. She pushed off her slippers with each foot and tucked her feet up underneath her.

Niki felt far away from them in her chair. She put her drink down and leant back in her seat, folding her arms across her chest as though hugging herself to keep warm. She wasn't ready for this woman to come in and start holding Damien's hand, smiling at her in that warm, generous sort of way.

'So, Nikita,' Dilani said, her eyes wide with friendliness. 'This must all feel very strange.'

Niki didn't answer.

'We're glad you're here,' Damien said again. 'I can't believe how grown-up you are!'

'Do you remember me?'

'Of course he does!'

'I was asking him.'

There was an awkward silence.

'Yeah, I do. I remember you. I remember everything. . . Well, OK, that's not strictly true. The thing you've got to understand is that I was in a really bad way by the time you and your mum left. And so there are certain things that were passing me by.

'I can't say we were happy or that things were particularly good . . . but taking all of that in, there's still lots I do remember very clearly. I remember that I loved you very much.'

'Did you love her? Mum?'

'I. . .'

Niki watched the smile on Dilani's face become more forced. Good, she thought.

'There was a time when, yes, I would say that I loved her. At least, I thought so. But as I've said, I messed up *everything*. For the most part I wasn't in a place, you know, where I *could* love her. I'm sorry. I have a lot of regret about that time. I was not good to her. I was not a good father to you.'

'Did you hit her?'

'Er, I'm not sure. . .' Dilani started to say, but Damien squeezed her hand and she stopped.

'Did she tell you that?' he asked.

'No. She won't talk about you. She says it was a really bad time and that we are safer without you, and to not think about you or talk about you because we are enough, me and her together, we're better off on our own.'

'And yet you've come to find me,' Damien said quietly.

'Yeah, well. . . I just found out and I. . .' her voice trailed off and she chewed on her lip.

'Look, this is a shock for both of us – *all* of us,' said Damien, when it became clear that Niki wasn't going to continue. 'I guess we just need to take our time, don't you think? We don't need to jump in with accusations or thrash out tonight *why* this and *how* that. Let's take our time to get our heads round it, yeah? I mean – that's if you want to see us again?'

Niki nodded.

'May I ask something?' Dilani said. 'Does your mum know that you're here?'

'Yes,' Niki said a bit too quickly.

'Perhaps we should speak to her,' Dilani said, looking at Damien.

'She doesn't want to talk to you.'

'I can understand that, but I just think—'

'Look. It's like . . . he . . . said, it all needs time. Don't go rushing in trying to call her, OK? She's said I can come, but she doesn't want anything to do with it.'

'Would she really send you off like that – to knock on the door of strangers?' Dilani said, but again Damien quietened her, patting her knees. 'I just think. . .' she muttered.

'OK,' Damien said. 'We'll leave it for tonight, but we can't leave it long. Agreed?'

'Whatever,' Niki said.

'Good. It's gone seven. Perhaps I should drive you home. We can arrange to meet again.'

'Tomorrow?'

'Er . . . how about the next day? The twenty-fourth.'

'Christmas Eve,' Niki said to no one in particular.

'Is that a problem?' Damien asked.

'No. What time?'

Damien and Dilani looked at each other, communicating silently.

'Why don't you come for lunch?' Dilani said, the warm, gentle smile back on her face, her eyes sparkling, looking completely black – impossible to distinguish iris from pupil. 'You and Damien – your dad – can have some time to talk, just the two of you, then you can have lunch with us and meet the girls. If you want.'

'Yeah. Fine.'

'Well, that's settled then,' Damien went to stand up.

'Just, Nikita. . .' Dilani said, untucking her feet and leaning forward, her elbows on her knees, her hands clasped together. 'Just so you know, we won't be explaining to the girls who you are – not just yet, OK? We need to work out exactly how we're going to do that. Damien and I will need time to talk it through, and then time to explain everything to them. I hope you'll respect our decision.'

'Fine. Whatever.'

'It's not to be unkind to you, but they're very young and it'll take a bit for them to understand . . . and we need to make sure. . .'

'I said fine. I mean – I don't mean to say it like that.' She tried again. 'It's *fine*, I understand.'

'Thank you.'

They all stood up. It was an awkward goodbye. Dilani patted her shoulder.

'See you again, Nikita.'

'People call me Niki,' she said, but couldn't quite bring herself to return Dilani's smile.

'Niki.' Dilani nodded. 'Well, see you.'

Damien strode out to the car and Niki could feel Dilani watching her from the front door.

'We'll have to wait for the engine to warm up before I can turn the heaters on, I'm afraid,' he said, blowing his hands and rubbing them together.

The narrow beams from the headlights tunnelled into the darkness ahead – drizzle seemed suspended in the light like dust motes.

He's not a murderer. He's not a murderer . . . but he is a real killer.

Niki imagined their car now ploughing into a person. Like those TV adverts warning against speeding where a dummy gets flung over the roof of a car and smashes onto the road. She imagined hearing the sound of a body colliding with the bonnet.

She wondered how often he thought about it. Could he remember the expression on the man's face? Had their eyes met at that startling moment of impact? Did he remember how the body had looked afterwards lying in the road, limbs jutting at impossible angles? Did he stop and try to get the man breathing again, trying not to notice the smashed back of skull, the dead-and-gone eyes, maybe a final bubble of breath popping on his bloody lips? Or did he simply drive away?

'So . . . this has all been quite the surprise,' Damien said. She could tell he was stuck for things to say but she didn't want to help him out. She wanted him to feel awkward, she realised.

'And are you at school here?'

'Tooting Comp.'

'That's where your mum went.'

'Yeah.'

He asked her how she was finding it, what her grandad was like, what she thought of Tooting. She mumbled her answers, but then suddenly worried whether he'd tell her he didn't want her to come for lunch if she was going to be like this. She chewed her lip and felt a prickle of tears at the corners of her eyes. He hadn't looked for her in all this time, so why would he want her to come for lunch? Why would he want her getting in the way of his neat, pretty family?

As they started along Bickersteth Road, near the turn off to her own, she said, 'You can drop me here.'

'I should take you to the door.'

'Please.'

'Nikita. Niki. Angie needs to know.'

'I *know*. Look, it's just – Hyacinth and I talked. *She* knows. I think it's going to be really weird for my mum. . . *You're* taking time to tell your daughters.'

'That's different.'

'Please.'

He pressed his hands on the top of his head, as though trying to squeeze out the right decision. 'I really don't know, Niki. . .'

'Just till after Christmas.'

He turned in his seat, holding onto the headrest behind her.

'OK. This is weird for all of us, isn't it? But I'm glad you've found me. I hope you believe me. I'm glad you turned up. It's just . . . well, we've all got to be a bit patient with each other, yeah?'

'Yeah.'

'OK, good.' He smiled, then looked a little unsure – as though he was thinking about kissing her goodbye.

Niki opened the car door quickly and got out.

'I'll wait here till I see you safely inside.'

As Niki opened the front door she paused to wave. Damien's car flashed its lights then headed off down the road. She watched until he had disappeared from view.

# FOURTEEN

'You haven't been round much,' Auntie Sita said, wagging a finger near to Niki's face.

'Sorry. I've been busy, Auntie.'

'*Busy!* Rude girl!'

Sangeeta smiled and rolled her eyes.

'Fine. I'll go,' said Sita, paddling her hands underneath her hair to fluff it up. 'I'll leave you to your chin-wagging gossipy chat. Here I am, babies, babies and now you send me away. The only bit of interest and I'm not invited. No respect. None. Fine. I must go iron, go jiggle babies on my knees – one on *each*. And you two just sit there like *heiresses*, like. . .' She left the room, her voice echoing down the hall.

Sangeeta laughed and shook her head. 'The holidays are the worst time because there's nowhere to go. *She* feels stuck here – what about me? But at least it is a time when I don't have to get up in the night.

'So, where *have* you been? You've hardly answered any of my texts. I think you see a lot of Chantelle.'

'A bit,' Niki shrugged. She'd had her first lunch with her dad and his family on Christmas Eve. On Christmas Day she hadn't seen them, but yesterday and the day before she'd been round both afternoons.

'Have you told your mum yet?' Dilani asked each time as she kissed Niki goodbye.

'Have you told Suki and May?'

'It's not the same, and you know it.'

But it still seemed to work in delaying them, Niki found.

'So here's everything I've done,' said Sangeeta, pushing over a pile of her work for Niki to take away and copy.

'Thanks,' Niki said.

'You've still got quite a few days to work.'

'Yeah. It's just – I'm quite busy.' She saw Sangeeta pursing her lips and added, 'Sorry I haven't seen more of you this holiday.'

'Well, why not come tomorrow with Raima, Kakali and me – we're going to KFC and then the cinema. It's going to be *great*, the first time . . . well, if you must know, it's the first time I've been allowed to do something like this. The cinema!'

'I'm sorry, I can't. And, actually, I should go.'

'Why can't you see me and Chantelle at the same time? Why don't you invite us to your house this holiday? Are you embarrassed by me? I'm not like your other friends – Tyrone and Janaia.'

'Jan*aia*'s not my friend!'

'Chantelle, then.'

'It's not about you and Chantelle. I can't have people over – my grandad's ill,' Niki mumbled, feeling slightly sick at herself. 'I'm not going to see her now, anyway. I've just got stuff to do.'

'Fine.'

'I'll arrange something, OK? We'll do something all together.'

'Whatever. See you at *school*,' said Sangeeta, even though there were still six days of the holidays left. Niki didn't promise otherwise.

♦♦♦♦

'I hope I did the right thing,' Angie said, staring out of the window at the rain. It was only three days after Boxing Day but she was feeling itchy to pull down the tired-looking decorations and get rid of the tree.

Robert put down his newspaper to listen to her. He found that it was best to wait and then usually the rest of her sentences would come after a pause.

'Not visiting Peter and Bea this holiday,' she explained. 'I think it would have been too soon. Niki needs to settle here.'

'I'm sure you've done the right thing.'

'We've hardly seen her all holiday!'

Now we're getting to it, Robert thought. He could almost feel Betsy smiling beside him. At last you're seeing how it's done.

'Well, that's what it's like round here,' he said. 'People don't go away. They don't have family to visit in other parts of the country – so that means Niki's got all these friends around to see. This is her settling in,' he said, shaking his newspaper open again.

Question resolved, he thought. Simple.

'I suppose so. . . I'm just not used to her being able to go *off* like this.'

Robert laid his paper again on his knees, folding it quietly and smoothing it with the palms of his hands.

'All her friends on her doorstep, rather than me having to *take* her places. She just comes and goes. . .'

'Uses the place like a hotel,' Robert said with a smile.

Angie looked over at him, recognising the phrase from his lectures when she was younger.

'Yes, well,' she said dryly. 'Is this what happens? Suddenly your child becomes a stranger?'

'And you just hope it doesn't last forever. That seems to be the form. Do you know, I don't think there was such a thing as a "teenager" when I was that age.'

'She's only fourteen.'

'They start younger and younger these days – getting older and older. Eventually they'll be coming out of the womb with driver's licences.'

Angie smiled at her dad using the word 'womb' in front of her. She had always seen him as one of those sorts who liked to pretend the human race didn't have bodily functions.

He liked that – they smiled at each other these days, they met each other's eyes. She had his eyes, the same watery blue.

They'd had an enjoyable Christmas. Probably, he supposed, because they'd all been anticipating something anti-climatic. But as it was, they had laughed a lot, the three of them sitting round the kitchen table wearing their paper crowns and making a pathetically small dent into the turkey that was meant to serve eight.

'Why on earth I bought one so big. . .' Angie had laughed, shaking her head.

They'd played Boggle and watched the afternoon film. Robert had insisted that they watch the Queen's speech first, and stand for the national anthem.

'Up you get, my girl,' he'd said tapping Niki on the back until she finally dragged herself up with a groan. Robert had caught Angela giving Niki a smile that said *humour him* and he had felt his heart swell. *This* was what he'd been hoping for. How he had longed at that moment to squeeze Betsy's hand.

♦♦♦♦

'It's called "Reespek" – which is kinda Jamaican for "respect" . . . which is kinda obvious,' Damien laughed. 'Anyway, so we get alongside the boys and we try and help them see they need to respect themselves, make something of this life, and that. . . Seeing as I got into drugs and stuff . . . well, I now give something back through this project, you know? I've been doing it ever since I got out. I was visited by this community worker while I was inside, and he knew about the project and so fixed me up with it. I started by doing odd jobs at times when the place was closed to kids, not having anything to do with the boys – painting, fixing things. But then gradually I was sent on courses – football coaching, leadership. . .

'We run loads of stuff for them. Sports, life skills, help with homework, all of that. And there's a youth club for them to hang out in, with pool tables and PlayStations.'

Niki lay on the carpet in Damien's living room, stretched out on her front, face cupped in her hands, propped up on her elbows so she could stare at her father who was lying along the full length of the sofa, his hands behind his head and his feet dangling over the end.

She loved how she only had to ask her dad a simple question – what do you do? what's your favourite food? how long have you lived here? – and then he would just talk and talk and talk. Her mum always clammed up when she asked a question, but her dad seemed to open like those gates she'd seen on canals where the water poured through, lifting up a boat.

And she was the boat.

Dilani was out sales shopping with Suki and May.

'What about girls?' Niki asked. 'Is there a project for them?'

'Well. That's a good point. But you know, it's boys that cause the most trouble. Boys are *twice* as likely to bunk school. Afro-Caribbean boys are the *worst*, although apparently white boys are catching up. It's like lads just see gang life as the only way – and for them there's no point, no *credibility* in doing well in school. That's *got* to change! These boys need to be able to get jobs, *good* jobs. They need to learn *reespek*. For themselves, for education, for hard work, for families – for women. They need to take *responsibility* and that means having respect and appreciation for others as well as themselves.

'Now girls, I grant you, need support too. But we can't do everything, you know? This particular project focuses on boys. I'm sure there's good stuff out there for girls. I know of a dance and drama project, for example, but this is what *I* know about – the lads.

'I've seen the damage that can be done – I've experienced it first-hand. So I can talk in language they understand. And I can *show* them that it's possible to make different choices.'

Wow, Niki thought. Her dad wasn't just *not* a criminal – he was totally amazing! Out there, saving young people from destruction. The readjustment of her father in her mind was like a blast of sunlight straight into the eyes. Dazzling.

'We're home!'

Niki hadn't heard the front door.

'Oh, hello, Niki. Here again?' said Dilani, her head

peeping round the side of the sitting room door.

'Is that a problem?'

'No, of course not! Will you stay for tea?'

'No. I have to get back.'

The girls ran in and leapt on their father, who curled inwards at the sudden elbows in his stomach as they clambered on top of him.

Dilani fell down into an armchair, laying her arms straight out along the armrests and her legs stretched out in front.

'It was absolutely *heaving*. It might have to be takeaway tonight, hon, unless you fancy cooking?'

Niki watched Dilani while trying to pretend that she wasn't.

'I should go.' She stood and waited. She supposed she wanted them to insist she stayed, even though she knew she couldn't.

'Well, you take care,' Dilani said, giving her usual broad smile, looking right into her eyes.

Outside she turned back. Damien had followed her to the front door and stood there waving while Dilani looked through the sitting room window, arms folded across her body, unsmiling. Suki and May had clambered onto an armchair and were waving energetically next to their mother.

♠♠♠♠

Niki made sure she could be round at her dad's the following afternoon for tea.

The girls skipped in and out of the kitchen, dressed up in their mother's scarves.

'Mum.' Suki entered, slipping along in her mother's shoes, holding a crumpled sheet of paper in her hands. 'How do you spell Nikita?'

'Well, why don't you ask Niki herself?'

'N-I-'

'You have to say it phonetically – do the sounds. Nuh, ih, kuh. . .'

Niki spelt out her name while Suki laboriously scored wobbly letters onto her drawing.

'It's for you,' she said after she'd finished, handing it to Niki and then slopping out of the kitchen again.

'Are you looking forward to school starting?' Dilani asked.

''S'orite.'

'Ugh, I'm dreading it!'

Dilani was a primary school teacher. Niki could imagine her clucking over her class as if they were her brood of little chicks, sheltering them under her long arms, her bracelets jangling against each other.

Niki never knew how Dilani would look when she arrived. Sometimes she was adorned with a richly-coloured scarf wrapped around her head. Or otherwise she left her head uncovered, her curls close to her scalp as though she didn't need the smoke and mirrors of elaborate hairstyles to trick people into finding her pretty.

She finished peeling the carrots that she'd been given to do, and wondered what her mum would look like with a patterned scarf wrapped around her head.

Upstairs, she could hear the girls arguing. Each had her own room, decorated with strings of lights that looked like pink and white flowers. Gauzy canopies had been screwed into the ceilings above their beds, Suki's white, May's pink. Each had the wall-side of their beds lined with cuddly toys and dolls with hair that could be brushed. Suki's duvet was a patchwork of fuchsia, turquoise and yellow, while May's had an enormous picture of Cinderella Barbie.

Niki loved cuddling them. They still didn't know who she was exactly but seemed to take it for granted that she came round most days. They would lean back against her when they sat on her lap to listen to stories, fighting for this prime spot, so that Dilani would come in and say, 'One on each side if you can't take it in turns.'

'Are you coming tomorrow?' they'd say and Niki would hear Dilani's knife pause in the kitchen.

'Sure,' she'd answer, then hear the chopping resume.

♦♦♦♦

Damien came home later than usual at the moment because of a holiday project being run at the youth club. Niki had helped to feed and bathe the girls and they were now watching television, but as soon as they heard him call, 'Anybody home?' they leapt up and ran from the room.

'Daddyyyy!'

'Umph!' Niki knew that was the sound of them running head first into him. 'Help! I'm being attacked!'

She went and watched from the sitting room door. Each time she saw him again she felt a little flip in her stomach and a rush of butterflies. When he smiled and said hello to her, she felt her cheeks go hot and was glad she didn't blush.

He had mud spattered up his trouser legs and flecked across his face.

'We went on an assault course today. Absolutely shattering. This is when I feel my age, I tell you. I'm going to be *stiff* tomorrow.'

Dilani came in, wiping her hands on a tea towel.

'You are *filthy*! Go take a bath, I'll bring you a cup of tea. The girls have eaten already and are all washed.'

'So I see,' he said drumming May's candy-striped bottom with both hands.

'Come on, girls, bedtime,' Dilani said. 'Say goodnight to Niki.'

'*Oh* – it's too *earlyyyy*!'

They each hugged Niki.

'You will be here tomorrow, won't you?'

'Definitely.'

'Quickly, girls.' Dilani followed them upstairs.

Damien sat down in a chair.

'Phew, I'm done in.'

'Shall I get you a cup of tea?' Niki said

'What I could do with is a juice. Thanks, hon.'

The little word of affection caused a tiny explosion inside her like a delicate firework, glowing with golden warmth.

When she brought back a glass of orange juice he was pulling something out of the pocket of his jacket, which was balled in a heap on the floor next to him.

'Niki, just while the others are upstairs. . . I got you a present. I mean, we've just had Christmas and

I didn't give you anything. I bought it, actually, the day after you first visited. I wanted to give it to you the next time you came, you know, on Christmas Eve when you came for lunch? I thought you could open it on Christmas Day, but then I thought it might be too soon.'

Niki nodded, still standing in front of him with the glass of orange juice in her hand.

'So . . . swap?' he smiled, reaching out with the present in one hand and opening his other for the glass of juice.

'I didn't get you anything,' she said.

'No, and you shouldn't. It's too early for presents, really – I hope you don't think that I think presents make up for anything.'

Out of a small plastic bag Niki pulled a tiny box and knew immediately that it must be jewellery. Inside the box was a delicate silver chain carefully laid onto a black spongy cushion. On the centre of the cushion lay a silver N. It had a sparkly stone in the top corner of the end stroke that looked to Niki just like a diamond.

'I hope you like it. I didn't know what to get you.'

'I love it.'

'Here, I'll help you put it on.'

She turned around so Damien could fasten the necklace.

'Now, let's take a look at you.'

She straightened the necklace and looked up at her father, who rested his hands on her shoulders.

'Nikita.' He drew her into a hug. 'I am very proud to know you. I can't quite believe that you're real.'

She could hear his voice shaking. She stood in his hug, not putting her arms around him, but trying not to be too stiff. She still found herself very shy with him.

'Whatever I can do to make up for the past I will try to do it, OK?'

The door banged open.

'Oops, sorry,' Dilani said. She had come in with a cup of tea and a packet of biscuits. 'I've got you some tea.'

'Oh, it's OK, thanks, Niki got me a juice.'

'Oh, well. Great.'

Niki saw Dilani's eyes fall on her necklace, and automatically her fingers went up to touch it. Dilani looked at Damien.

'I got Nik a present,' he said.

'It's very pretty. Damien, why don't you go take a bath, you stink.'

He laughed and approached her with his muddy arms outstretched, 'Hug me!' but Dilani moved aside, batting at him with the packet of biscuits and shooing him out of the room like she did with the girls.

'Are you heading off now?' she said to Niki.

'It's OK, I can stay for dinner.'

'It's just that Damien might be a while and dinner isn't ready yet. I don't want to make you late.'

'It's OK. It's still the holidays so I can be out a bit later. Mum isn't expecting me home for a while yet.' Niki sat down and looked at the television again.

'OK. Well. I'll go add some more rice, shall I? Right. More rice. You make yourself at home.'

♠♠♠♠

Niki picked apart the pastry around her McDonald's apple pie until her fingers touched hot apple sauce. She pressed down and watched the filling ooze out through the small hole onto a paper napkin.

Chantelle sucked her milkshake noisily through her straw.

'Stuff's too fick to get fru dis fing,' she said, screwing up one eye to look down the straw as though she might find a solution.

Sangeeta spun her small cup of lemonade on the

table and delicately ate her French fries, taking several bites over each one.

'I can't believe I'm eating McDonald's,' she said. Her face glowed like she'd won the lottery, Niki thought. 'KFC *and* McDonald's all in the same week!'

'Oh my days,' muttered Chantelle, shaking her head and looking as if she was trying to hide from public view. 'I'm in 'ere like every *day* man and you talkin' like it's de most amazin' fing on dis planet. Whatchu on?'

Niki nibbled some pastry. She usually loved these apple pies but her stomach felt full with the discomfort of her two friends so evidently not getting on. She chewed her straw and tried to think of something they could all talk about and agree on. Her mind was utterly blank.

'So whatchu doin' for New Year's?' Chantelle asked her.

Niki shrugged. 'Dunno.'

''Cause, right, dere's gonna be a par'y. Some girl in Year Eleven is 'avin' it and my cousin is in 'er form and reckons she could get some of us in, right. In Clapham.'

Niki knew there was no way her mum would let her go.

'You are allowed to go to parties?' Sangeeta asked, and Niki wished that her accent sounded a little less . . . neat. She sounded every syllable with a precision that Beatrice Munroe would have commended. 'You'll be allowed out on New Year's Eve – until the next day?'

'Yeah, course. Where you *from* man?'

Niki just managed to stop herself from joining in with a scornful laugh. She felt torn between wanting to defend Sangeeta and not wanting to lose face in front of Chantelle. It was as if they were the two sides of herself in bodily form, splitting her loyalties right down the middle.

'There's no way I'll be allowed to go,' she said. 'No *way*.'

'Guess not, neek,' grinned Chantelle. 'And, well, if you must know,' she said to Sangeeta, 'I'm telling my mum I'm staying at a friend's an' den my cousin is gonna take me along. She'd probably flip – my cousin, dat is – if I turned up wiv loads of you, anywayz, so it's probably for de best. . . An' my mum would freak if she knew.' Chantelle grinned, 'It's gonna be *great*! And Tyrone's gonna be dere. . .' she added, singing his name and giving Niki a nudge.

'That boy's trouble,' said Sangeeta.

'Oi, you, watch it. Dat's my cousin you're talkin' 'bout.'

'Well, Chantelle, that doesn't change the fact that it's true.'

'S'pose.' She grinned at Niki. 'She's a right one, dis girl of yours. "That boy is trouble!"' she said mimicking Sangeeta's voice. 'Just fink,' she sighed, 'you could of kissed Tyrone under de mistletoe.'

'That's Christmas, fool.'

'Who you callin' fool, *fool*?'

Sangeeta laughed. 'Takes one to know one, doesn't it?'

Chantelle shouted a laugh. 'Cheeky cow!'

Niki found herself starting to relax.

# FIFTEEN

Niki sat in front of the television, waiting for fireworks to explode over the London Eye. All she could think about was Chantelle being at a proper party. Teenagers having a house party together, while she sat on the sofa next to her mum who was wearing tracksuit bottoms and a fleece. Grandad had gone to bed at ten o'clock.

'This is *boring*.'

'The fireworks won't be long now – it's nearly midnight.'

'This man's boring.'

'He is a bit. Does it every year. An institution.'

'I bet you didn't used to spend New Year's Eve sitting in with *your* parents.'

'Oh, I get it,' said Angie, laughing. 'What you're saying is that *I'm* boring. Charming.'

'I'm just saying, like, I bet you spent New Year's with your friends.'

'Yes, and look where I ended up. . . Actually,' Angie mused, 'when I was little – ten or twelve-ish – we used to go to these family parties – parents and children, all together. Dad used to *hate* it. Mum'd dance the night away.'

'Why couldn't we of 'ad one of those?'

'"Couldn't we of 'ad?" Where did you learn to speak?'

Niki scowled and flicked channels. She knew that Damien and Dilani had got babysitters in so that they could go to a party. Maybe they would have let her go along if she'd asked.

'We'll miss the fireworks, love, if you keep hopping about.'

'Who *cares*, anyway? It's all *boring*.'

'Well, Niki, I'm sorry that life is dealing you such a rough hand. That you have to spend a night somewhere warm, having had a decent meal, with a comfy bed to go to, having a mother who loves you and looks after you, having just been given all these presents for Christmas. . .'

'All *right*. Oh my days, man, talk about overreacting.'

It's like an alien has taken possession of my daughter, Angela thought. She chewed the insides of her cheeks to stop herself saying anything else that made her sound just like her father.

♠♠♠♠

Niki awoke. She rolled to one side and realised that when she'd gone to bed last night, straight after the fireworks, climbing the stairs with her eyes practically closed, she had fallen into bed without turning on her night light. She smiled to herself as she turned onto her back and stared at the ceiling. She didn't need night lights any more.

She got up and ate breakfast in her pyjamas.

'Happy New Year,' said Grandad, who'd already cleared away all the breakfast things. 'How are you going to fit in your lunch if you're eating that chocolate cereal at a quarter to twelve, hey?'

Niki smiled at him through a mouthful of Coco Pops and Grandad shook his head with a smile that said he would never understand the youth of today.

'Foof!' Angie came into the kitchen and stood resting her hands on her knees, red faced and sweating. 'It's so funny, *everybody's* out there. New Year's resolutions – all of us puffing round the park like we're going to drop dead at any second. Probably the one and only time some people will ever go.'

'Not you, though,' said Robert.

'No,' said Angie. 'It is definitely time I got in shape. I'm only thirty, for crying out loud. It's time I stopped behaving like a granny. No giving up for me.'

'That's my girl.'

Niki texted Sangeeta and Chantelle to wish them a Happy New Year. Sangeeta texted back inviting her over.

She hadn't arranged to see Damien and his family today and wondered about calling them. She wasn't sure what time people got up after New Year's parties.

'Can I go round to Sangeeta's?' she asked, thinking she could do that and then see if she could go round to her dad's a bit later.

'Why not invite her here?' Angie asked. 'I wouldn't want your friends to think they aren't welcome – you always seem to go to them.'

'It's just easier for Sangeeta 'cause she sometimes looks after the baby,' Niki said, thinking it would be much harder for her to add on a visit to her dad's if she invited Sangeeta over, rather than getting out of the house herself.

'Is that poor girl ever given a moment of rest?'

'It's only, like, if her auntie needs to nip to the shops or summink.'

'What *would* Bea say if she heard you speak these days?' Angie said dryly.

'Can I go, then?'

'Yes, love. Get dressed and then let's work out a time for you to be back.'

'What about lunch?' Grandad asked.

'Coco Pops!'

♦♦♦♦

'She's not answering,' said Niki, staring at her phone.

Sangeeta carried on folding the salwar kameez that she had just finished ironing, plucking at any creases with her fingers and smoothing it over with the palms of her hands.

'Well, she obviously had fun at the party. Maybe she's still sleeping.'

Niki knew she was being rude – all she'd done since arriving at Sangeeta's was talk about Chantelle. She wasn't sure why she was like this to Sangeeta, but even though she knew she was being irritable and acting as though she didn't want to be here, she found it hard to behave differently.

It was just that, sitting around watching Sangeeta iron wasn't quite how she'd been hoping to spend the afternoon. Whenever she came round Sangeeta was always in the middle of something – or they were given chores to do together. Even if Sangeeta *had* managed to finish her jobs for the day, there was nowhere for them to go – they could only sit in the kitchen with people wandering in and out.

Occasionally, they went into Sangeeta's family's room. But it was dark in there, and weird sitting on the bed Niki knew Sangeeta's parents must sleep in. Sangeeta had a roll mat and sleeping bag that she tidied away each day under the bed. Niki couldn't help wondering what Sangeeta's parents did if they wanted to have sex. Did they just do it – and hope their daughter was asleep? She didn't like sitting on their bed having thought about them having sex.

And the room was so full of *stuff* – three people's worth of stuff. It just wasn't much fun sitting in that dingy room watching TV.

So usually she said she was happy sitting in the kitchen. While Sangeeta ironed this afternoon, Niki sketched in a notebook to keep herself occupied. Auntie Sita came in and scolded her for not doing something more productive.

'You should be revising or *doing* something, my girl. Sangeeta here is work work work. She'll make a good life for herself.'

'And me?'

'Well, dear. It's up to you – a job and a good life. Or single mother on benefits.'

Niki opened and closed her mouth but Sita was cooing to her baby, dancing with her out of the room.

'I'm sorry about my auntie.'

'Does she know I'm in all the top sets like you?'

'More than me. You're a set higher in Maths.'

'Yeah, well.'

'She just feels she has to make a point.'

'What point is that, exactly?'

'It's to me really. . . Look, she's worried you will be a bad influence. You know, lots of the black and mixed raced teenagers have a bit of a bad reputation round here. I'm sorry, it's just the way she sees it. And children from single-parent homes. Those sorts of things.'

Niki could feel herself opening and closing her mouth again.

'Me going for McDonald's with you and Chantelle – they get worried I'll stop working.'

'Because you ate some chips?'

'Well . . . you *have* stopped studying. You borrow my homework,' Sangeeta said quietly.

Niki looked at her. 'I'll give it back if it bothers you.'

'I didn't say that. I'm just . . . concerned.'

'Well, don't be, *Auntie* Sangeeta.'

'Niki.'

'Forget it.'

'Niki. Come on, don't be angry with me. You know what my auntie and parents are like. They need me to work as hard as I possibly can, you know all that. And I'm worried about you. You're so great at school but recently it's like you don't care – all this holiday, not working, never being around. And. . .' Sangeeta stopped and pressed her lips tightly together, trapping her words. She smiled apologetically, unplugged the iron and then began to put the ironing board away.

'Go on,' Niki said.

'Well, when we're with Chantelle – you're different. It's like you don't *like* me when we're with her. Why invite me along if you don't want me there?'

'Ugh,' Niki sighed and scribbled over her drawing. 'Of course I like you. It's just – you and Chantelle. Well, you're so different and sometimes I sort of feel stuck in the middle.'

'I embarrass you. Show you up.'

'That's not what I said.'

Sangeeta coiled the flex around the iron.

'Let's go do something else. Not talk about this.'

'Sangeeta.'

'Honestly, I understand.' She smiled. 'Come on, let's go buy something from the shop round the corner – then go back to your house?'

'All right,' Niki said. 'I'm not embarrassed by you,' she added, and determined never to be again.

She texted her dad to ask if she could visit tomorrow instead and listened to Sangeeta softly asking permission to go out from her mother. When Mrs Devarajah came to say goodbye, Niki made sure she sounded extra polite – as though she were a good influence.

As soon as they stepped outside into the afternoon light it felt as though their argument was left behind. They smiled and started planning what to buy at the shops, deciding to make hot chocolate with marshmallows in it.

'And that squirty cream stuff,' said Niki, linking arms with Sangeeta.

They slowed down at the sight of a police car outside Chantelle's house.

'What should we do?' Niki asked.

'What *can* we do? They probably can't have visitors.'

'I'll call her.' Niki rang Chantelle's phone. There was no answer but then Sangeeta pointed and they saw Chantelle looking down from her bedroom. She stood like a ghost mingled into the sky that was reflected on the window. Chantelle pointed along towards the end of the road.

'Come on,' said Niki. 'She'll come round the back.'

They ran to the end of the street and waited. Chantelle appeared wearing the black bandana that she always slept in, an oversize sweatshirt and leggings, and a white woollen scarf coiled round and round her neck.

'What's wrong? What's happened?' Niki asked as soon as Chantelle was close enough to hear them. Chantelle kept walking until she was right in front of them.

'Hi, Gee'a,' she said and gave such a sad smile that Niki felt a pang of terror. She'd never seen Chantelle like this before.

Chantelle looked down at her feet.

'Last night. At de party. Well, not at it, but nearby, yeah. . . Tyrone got stabbed.'

*'What?'*

'He's in 'ospital. Dey got 'im just once – just *once* – in de leg and e's, like, critical.'

Chantelle was crying, her eyes puffy and bloodshot.

'Is he. . . I mean . . . he's going to be all right?'

'Dey don't know yet. He lost a lot of blood, see. But 'e's a fighter, innit, so. . .'

'I'm sure he'll pull through, Chantelle,' said Sangeeta, reaching out and squeezing her arm.

As Chantelle looked at Sangeeta, tears began running down her cheeks. Sangeeta took the end of Chantelle's scarf and wiped her face. She suddenly looked younger to Niki. No longer this friend she was trying to live up to, always two steps ahead, their age difference seeming cavernous. Now she seemed just like a girl, just like them.

'Oh, Chan.'

'It was 'is *own* stupid bloody Stanley knife. Dey stabbed 'im wid 'is own freakin' knife!'

'But not actually *at* the party?'

'Nah, he left to go meet some mates. I dunno. 'E must of gone into de wrong area. Went where some gang didn't recognise 'im. Or 'e didn't know the right words to get fru or summink. I didn't know anyfing about it till dis mornin'. He didn't come 'ome and den de police went round my auntie's and she just totally collapsed, man. She's at ours now. She was at de 'ospital but dey sent 'er 'ome and said dey'd call when dere's any change. It's a complete mess. Everyone's goin' out of deir minds. My mum's goin' in la'er but de police are round questionin' us and dat.'

Niki didn't know what to say. There was nothing to say.

'Bet you're glad you didn't come, hey?' Chantelle said, only managing to pull one side of her mouth into a smile. 'It were rubbish, anyway. Everyone was wasted before dey even arrived – Tyrone was off 'is 'ead when 'e left. My cousin went off wiv some bloke and I was just like *dere*, not knowin' anyone, lookin' like an idiot. It were crap.'

Sangeeta stepped forward and put her arm round Chantelle's shoulders.

'I should get back before dey miss me.'

She hugged them both.

'Let us know what's happening,' Niki said.

'Yeah.'

They watched her go, head down, arms pinned to her side. Niki remembered Chantelle seeing her home after Tyrone had threatened her with that same knife. The way she'd walked then had made Niki imagine her taking off into the air.

⁂

'You're late,' Suki and May said with accusing frowns the following day.

'Well, I'm here now. And I'll be here tomorrow.'

'I thought school started tomorrow,' Dilani said.

'I'll come after.'

Niki watched Dilani turn away to the sink and turn on the tap in a way that expressed a tightened jaw, a breath held in.

She attempted to be helpful, picking up a used chopping board to put in the dishwasher, thinking it would be best to keep her on side, and realising that she hadn't been trying particularly hard.

'Leave those, I'll do it,' Dilani said with a smile, while not looking directly at her.

Niki felt a slight pull as she tried to keep hold of the board.

'It's OK, I'll put it in the—' but already Dilani had drawn it out of her hands.

'Why don't you join the others next door?'

Again the megawatt smile – the beaming spotlight. But it was fixed there, Niki could see. She mirrored back this showing of teeth, the pulling back of lips into something that was in danger of becoming a sneer rather than a smile.

In the other room, she found the girls pulling a doll, head pointing down so its hair of plaited wool hung towards the carpet, legs akimbo, stretched to the point where she could hear the stitching tear.

'Care*ful*! You'll *rip* it!'

''S not *fair*! I had it *first*!'

'It's *MINE*!'

Dilani came in at the sound of shrieking, took the toy and said, '*Neither* of you is going to have it if you're going to behave like that. What will Niki think, hmm? That's not how we behave now, is it? What do you say?'

'Sorry, Niki,' they chorused.

Niki felt embarrassed and cut off. The guest. The one to behave in front of. She flashed a scowl at Dilani, who was already leaving the room.

When Damien came in the whole household visibly brightened and relaxed.

'My giiiirrrrrlssss!' He ran in and scooped up his daughters. Dilani stepped forward and Niki watched as he kissed her on the mouth. Properly. No dry, screwed-up lips, but a long, full kiss that made Niki look away.

'Niki! Good to see you,' Damien said, looking up and seeing her standing further along the hallway. He stepped forward and, to her surprise, kissed her on the temple.

'I see you're wearing your necklace,' he said.

'Shall I get you a drink, or will Niki do it?' Dilani said.

'Tea would be great,' replied Damien, heading on into the kitchen. 'Anyone else?' he asked as he lifted the kettle to check it had enough water and then turned it on. 'You will never guess what Jaden said today, right. . . He was foolin' on the wall outside the club, yeah. . .'

Niki stood in the hallway. She wanted to run in and fling her arms around him, be held by her dad, have him kiss her again, have him hold her head to his chest the way he did with his little girls, whispering silly things into their ears that only they could hear.

She went to stand in the kitchen doorway, watching Dilani putting a tea bag into a cup while Damien sat down at the kitchen table, looking tired as he untied his trainers. The girls crowded in to show him the paintings they'd done that day.

He looked up and saw Niki standing there.

'Hey, Niki, so, last day of the holidays, huh? You're looking a bit miserable.'

'Yeah.'

Damien laughed, 'I'm sure it's not that bad.'

She could feel Dilani's eyes on her but didn't look at her.

'But you're doing pretty well, yeah?'

'I'm doing all right.'

Last night she'd copied all of Sangeeta's homework, feeling horribly guilty and vowing never to do it again. The fact Sangeeta had been so nice and willing to lend it to her made her feel even worse. Angie kept asking what she was doing upstairs but all she'd wanted to do was lie on her bed and copy words without thinking what they meant, keeping her phone next to her in case Chantelle texted with any news about Tyrone.

'Oh, love, we'll hear something soon,' Angie told her when she brought up a sandwich for Niki's dinner. She hadn't eaten it, and that night she slept with her night light on again.

'Well, mind you keep going,' Damien continued. 'It's important. What are you going to do when you grow up?'

'I don't know . . . maybe . . . you know, social work or something. Help people make the most of their opportunities.'

'Like father, like daughter,' said Dilani quietly. 'So, I guess you should be heading back for supper?' she said a little more loudly. 'Last night and all – see a bit of your mum.'

'No it's OK, I can stay, thanks.'

'Are you sure? Your poor mum and grandad. They can hardly be seeing you these days.'

'They're all right. I was there last night.'

'Hope you're not sick of chicken and rice!' said Damien.

'I love it.'

'Well, that's settled then,' said Dilani. 'Would you do me a huge favour and just keep an eye on the girls for half an hour? Play with them upstairs? It'd be such a help.'

Niki felt she had no choice. She wanted to talk to her dad about Tyrone, but there didn't seem the opportunity. Maybe when Dilani put the girls to bed a bit later.

Dilani had already turned so that she blocked Damien from Niki's view and had begun talking to him.

'So, what will happen with Jaden then, I mean if he. . .'

Niki took the girls upstairs to play with their Bratz, – hideous, pug-faced dolls with caked on make-up and thick, plasticky hair.

'I'm calling my doll Niki!' laughed Suki. 'We're

playing Mums and Dads – who do you want to be?'

Niki sat on the bed. 'I'll just watch, thanks.'

'Ohhhhh! Can't you be the grandma or something? Or the dog?'

'I'll be. . . your next door neighbour. But I'm at home eating my tea right now, so you can't see me.' She sat on the bed and pulled the canopy around her.

'May, you'll have to be the dog then.'

'Who's the daddy?'

'I'll be the mummy *and* the daddy.'

''S not *fair*!'

Niki leant back against the wall and watched the two girls acting out their game. Suki bossed May through every little scene and then made them repeat it until she felt it was right.

She watched them in a daze, smiling each time they looked up for her approval. They didn't seem to mind the tone of voice she said things in as long as she said them. 'Oh, how *nice* of my neighbours to drop in these *flowers*. *And* an invite to tea! I can't *wait* to go!'

'OK, it's tomorrow, so you're here now for tea,' said Suki, looking impatient.

'I'll just go see how long till your mum wants to give you your baths,' Niki said finally, sure that more than half an hour had gone by.

On the stairs, Niki could hear Damien and Dilani's voices from the kitchen.

'I'm just *saying*!'

'Look, she's a *kid* – she's not going to be thinking about the etiquette of it all. I mean, what even *is* the correct form? She has only just found me – found *us* – of course she's going to want to be here a lot!'

'Damien, I get that. I'm not trying to be unwelcoming. But – just hear me out. Look, we are the adults in this, OK? We're the ones who need to set the boundaries. We have the girls to think about.'

'They love her! They get on like a house on fire. I think it's really going to work. I mean, if you think about all the messed-up homes kids come from – this is *nothing* compared to that! One half-sister – big deal!'

'It *is* a big deal. We are a family – and I know, I *know* that she is now a part of that, is your daughter. Oh, come on, Damien, can't you see what I'm saying? She's here the *whole* time. *We* have to make this work – lay down the ground rules. Otherwise it'll get too intense and blow up in your face, I'm telling you.'

'That's why we're taking our time, Dila! That's *why* I'm not rushing in with "ground rules" – we're just letting this develop slowly—'

'There's nothing slow about it! Since she first knocked on the door, she's been here *every day* save about *two*! You're not even *here* half the time and she still comes round!'

'I can understand this is hard for you. But we did discuss—'

'Damien! I have always been ready for this, I'm not saying she's not welcome. Can't you just understand that this is a big change – that when the girls do finally understand who she is then this *will* rock them. They're fine now because they don't *know*. Why are you being so—'

'So *what*?'

'And her mother has *got to know*. It's been over two weeks! I know you're not looking forward to it—'

'You've no idea, Dila.'

'It's not fair on her. She's Niki's *mother*. She *has* to know – and the sooner she does—'

'The sooner you'll be rid of me,' Niki said, standing in the doorway. Dilani had been gesticulating at Damien with a wooden-handled fish slice, and stood with it frozen in mid-air. From where Niki stood it looked as though it would come straight down on Damien's head.

'Niki, please understand,' said Dilani.

'Oh, I understand. I heard everything.'

'Well, I think you've misunderstood me.'

'You were very clear,' said Niki, stepping into the room to pick up her coat from the back of a chair.

'Please don't go like this, Nikita,' Damien said. 'Dilani was just raising the question of telling your mother.'

'Only because she knows it'll end me being allowed to see you.'

'That's not true, Niki,' said Dilani.

'My friend got stabbed yesterday. He's in hospital. He might die.'

'I didn't know that,' Dilani said quietly. 'I'm very sorry.'

Niki could feel the tears welling up inside her. She zipped up her coat and headed out of the front door, slamming it shut in the middle of Damien calling her name.

# SIXTEEN

She ran down the first side street she saw, and then a different road again, trying to go a way that she thought they wouldn't be able to follow, arriving at a different bus stop to her usual one. She wanted to make them feel afraid.

It wasn't that she wanted to break up their family. She knew the girls – and Dilani – were his family now. She knew they were happy. But sometimes she found it hard not to imagine *her* mum in that kitchen making Damien a cup of tea, listening to his story about the boys he'd worked with that day. Suki and May were in that picture, and Niki was there, the eldest daughter, laughing with her parents – being a sort of mini-mum to the girls. It was just all minus Dilani. It wasn't personal. But she was the one stopping them becoming a family – the family they should always have been. All it was, Niki reasoned, was that her mum had been too young at the time. It had gone wrong because Damien had made mistakes and her mum had been too young. But he was OK now. And her mum was older.

She knew it was stupid and it made the tears come again. She could hear her mum's voice, 'Isn't this enough – just you and me? We're family.' But to Niki, family had always implied more than two.

And to have been so tremendously, wondrously surprised by how *great* her dad was. The way he cuddled his girls and played with them – splashed them during their bath times and set wind-up sea creatures scurrying along the floor of their bath so that they squealed and stood up, sending tidal waves of water onto the floor. And then he enveloped their glistening brown bodies in fluffy pink towels and squeezed the water out of their plaits.

She loved the little routines she was now establishing, tiny things that probably no one else noticed, minute traditions forming as hard and fast as she could make them happen, etching herself into the picture. She always took the same seat in the sitting room, she always used the same glass for her drink – a highball with daisies printed round the rim – she always said no thank you to carrots. Even though she didn't mind carrots, it made her smile inside to hear May say, 'Mu-um, she doesn't *like* carrots,' as though it was something they all knew.

After dinner, after the girls were tucked up in bed, her most special time was sitting with Damien watching TV for half an hour or so before he drove her home – side by side, right next to him on the sofa. He'd ask her some small question. Just an aside that didn't really matter. But that was it, the normality, the half-glanced attention that implied familiarity, permanence. And she would answer, trying to sound as casual as he did, trying to keep her eyes fixed on the television. She frequently had to remind herself not to stare, not to always turn her face and follow his every move like a sunflower trained on the sun.

She sat in the bus stop, waiting. She wondered what he'd do – phone her mum? Phone Hyacinth? Do nothing? Maybe right now Dilani was talking him out of having any more to do with her.

'Look at her, so ungrateful – we've let her into our home and all I do is make some innocent comment and *look* how she *overreacts*! We can't trust her. She wants to wreck our family. . .'

And he'd sit down again and nod his head sadly. 'I just wish she were more mature. Maybe in a couple more years. . .'

And then if she tried to go round he'd meet her at the door, bar her way, shake his head and say, 'Sorry, but my family must come first – and you. . . you are not in it.'

She imagined it all too vividly and had to brush away her tears when the bus finally arrived. Stepping on without looking at the driver, she took a seat right at the back on the bottom deck. It was easy to keep the tears flowing when she thought, too, about Tyrone – imagining him lying there with all those machines around him like she'd seen on *Casualty*, maybe Chantelle at his bedside. What if he *died*? She could see that yellow-handled Stanley knife, see its steel grey blade, imagine it being driven deep into his thigh.

Where should she go? She was on a bus back to Tooting because she didn't know anywhere else. She thought about not going home but knew it would only make everything worse. Her hope had to be that Damien and Dilani would leave things, give it all time to blow over. Then she could say sorry. She could talk to them and agree boundaries. There was still a chance it would all be OK.

She knew, however, that they would insist on speaking to her mum. And she just couldn't see any future in which she visited her dad with her mum knowing about it. How on earth would she tell her? How would she *start* the conversation? She thought about lying – pretending she'd only just found out about her dad, hadn't met him yet – but she knew it would be impossible. It was going to make it all a million times worse – that she'd been seeing him all through the Christmas holidays.

Opening the door as quietly as she could, she felt a strong temptation to disappear upstairs, put her head underneath her pillow and hope things would seem better later on.

'Nikita,' her mother called from the sitting room. There was something in her tone – a little too high-pitched, a little too shaky – that told her that it had already happened. She walked into the sitting room and found her mum holding sheets of her homework.

'I went to extract that uneaten sandwich from your room – and look what I found. . . Sangeeta's homework – and yours.'

Niki chewed her lip. So this was all it was, she thought, relieved.

'Don't you have anything to say? Nothing at all? Shall we sit down and have a little chat?'

Niki fell into an armchair. 'Where's Grandad?'

'Grandad has made himself scarce. Now, are you going to tell me what a bright girl like you is doing copying somebody else's homework?'

'Tyrone might *die* and you just care about some stupid homework.'

'I beg your pardon? I've had just about enough of this attitude. I know your friend is in a serious condition – and I am *very* sorry about it. We're all waiting, desperately hoping that that young boy will pull through. But that has nothing to do with this. Now, I've spoken to you in a respectful way, haven't I? Haven't I?'

'Yes.'

'Well. Please will you pay me the same courtesy? Love, I'm trying to be reasonable, but I don't want to see you squandering all your opportunities. It is simply unacceptable. . .'

'I won't do it again.'

'Why have you even done it *this* time? You've had all holiday! What have you girls been *doing* together?'

Robert knocked on the door frame by the kitchen entrance.

'Excuse me,' he said. 'I've only just realised that I'd left the phone off the hook, so this person wasn't able to get through before. It's for you,' he said looking at Angela. As he handed the phone to her his eyes flickered to meet Niki's and she knew immediately that it was Damien.

Her mum looked down at her, both her eyebrows rising towards her hairline as she listened.

'Just hold a minute please, I need to go somewhere quieter,' she said, walking out of the room into Robert's, closing the door behind her.

Robert stood looking at Niki for a moment.

'Mind if I turn on the box?' he said, sitting down beside her. Niki went to get up. 'Best if you stay here, I imagine, my girl. Face the music, don't you think?'

At the sound of his door opening again, some ten minutes later, Robert turned off the television and disappeared into the kitchen.

Angie came back into the room and sat down in a chair opposite Niki.

Niki knew there was nothing to say, nothing that could take away the look on her mother's face – the look of someone who'd cut their hand on broken glass.

'It's just taking a little while to sink in,' Angie said. 'Excuse me if I seem a little taken aback. At the thought of my daughter, for *weeks*—'

'Two weeks,' Niki interrupted.

'Oh. I'm sorry. Two weeks. Well, that's all right, then.'

'Mum.'

'What were you *thinking*? Do you have any idea how dangerous this could have been?'

'But he's OK! He's not dangerous – he's, like, normal!'

'That is for me to decide. I am your *mother*. Do you understand? *I* decide.'

'But you'd have said no!'

'I'm your mother.'

'Who cares?'

'Niki!'

'But you wouldn't have *let* me! I understand – he was horrible to you. He was into drugs. I know. But he's really sorry. He's totally different now – he's a really good person.'

Angie snorted through her nose and rolled her eyes – a childish gesture that made Niki despise her for a moment.

'He *is*! You've got to meet him and then you'll see.'

'The point is, Niki, that you lied.'

'You've lied to me about loads of things.'

'That's simply not true!'

'Grandma and Grandad.'

'I've been protecting you. It's not easy being a single parent, you know. I've had to make choices. I've always done the best for you.'

'But don't get so angry with me! I didn't do it to get at you or anything – I just wanted to know him. I'm *allowed* to see my dad!'

'The point, Niki, is your lying. Is your going out day after day, *lying*. Telling me you're one place, when you're somewhere completely different.

'You've started to dress differently. Your hair was only the start, now it's the way you speak, your clothes. . . You haven't done any of your schoolwork all holiday – you've *copied* someone *else's*! You're hardly here. . .'

Niki scowled and folded her arms.

'This move hasn't been good for you. You've changed beyond all recognition.'

'No I haven't!'

'You're insolent,' countered Angie, looking into Niki's defiant eyes. 'Secretive. And Tyrone – I mean, it's *dangerous* round here.'

'*You've* been all moody and quiet, too,' said Niki. 'And you hardly ever leave the house!'

'Don't speak to me like that.'

'This isn't *fair*!' shouted Niki, standing up. 'I just want to know my *dad* – it's not a crime!'

'What's that round your neck?'

As Niki had been throwing her arms about while she spoke, her silver N necklace had slipped over the collar of her jacket and was now swinging to and fro around her neck.

'Who gave you that?'

Niki rubbed it with her fingers and put it back inside her jacket.

'Presents! He's only known you five minutes! Don't you see?'

'It's not like that.'

Tears sprang up in Angie's eyes. She wiped her cheek angrily. Seeing the tears made Niki feel afraid.

'This place just isn't good for you.'

'Oh, come on, Mum!'

'I feel like I don't know you any more.'

'You *do*. It's just that I've found my dad. It doesn't change anything.'

'It changes everything!'

'You can't stop me seeing him. He's not a bad person – he's not like you think he is.'

'I'm not saying you can't see him. . . I'm just saying that this . . .' she gestured around her, 'Tooting . . . isn't working. It's not safe here. You were getting on so well in Oakley.'

'We can't go back there now!'

'You loved it there – you love the Munroes.'

'You can't *do* this! You say I can see Dad and then you say we have to move!'

'You'll still be able to see him, but we'll be in a better environment. Moving back to Oakley won't stop you seeing him.'

'It *will* and you know it! And what about Grandad?'

'He can come with us, or we can sort something out. I am *not* saying that you can't see your father. But I've let you run your own way for too long. Believe me, this is for your own good.'

'Mum, please don't do this!'

'I'm the one who's looked after you all your life. I'm your mother, Niki. You've got to remember that you are a child and you don't get to make the decisions yet.'

'But this is so unfair! Every time you find something hard you *move*. It's pathetic.'

'You're too young—'

'You don't ever *listen*! You say it's all about protecting me but that's rubbish – it's all about you.'

Niki turned from the room, ignoring her mother

telling her to 'get back here,' out through the front door, running as fast as she could. She could hear her mum calling after her, but again she was down a side street and then another, as fast as she could go.

♠♠♠♠

Here he was, in the sitting room. Taller than Robert remembered him. Robert hovered in the kitchen. Now that he'd been sent out by Angela – 'Please, Dad, go' – he was at a loss as to what to do. He'd phoned Hyacinth to put her on alert – hadn't told her the full ins and outs, just that Niki had run off a bit upset, if she turned up, please, to call. Nothing about it having to do with the father. He had no one else to call.

Angela had phoned Damien back after Niki ran off, and then some of the homes of Niki's friends. Robert had fluttered about behind her, until finally she'd flapped him away with her hands.

He said he'd be in the kitchen. He wanted to be on hand. Not that he'd be able to *do* anything of course. Call the police, he supposed, if it came to that.

But the man didn't seem likely to be violent – never really had, of course, on the few occasions Robert had met him, but he'd heard snippets from

Betsy after it had all finished. He was pretty sure he didn't know the half of it.

Angela had gone whiter than white when she opened the door to him. Damien had looked past her and started talking to him.

'Good evening, Mr Smith. I'm sorry to disturb you and can understand this must be difficult for you both – a bit sudden and everything.'

Robert had been holding his newspaper limp at his side. As he stood there, he realised that the buttons of his cardigan were done up incorrectly. He felt small and weak and foolish, as this man whom he'd despised for over a decade now spoke to him with confidence and, it seemed to Robert, with a sort of patronising respectfulness reserved for the elderly. This thought helped him gather himself and say, 'I suppose you'd better come in,' in his almost forgotten Maths-Teacher-Dad voice.

The father of his granddaughter, their little Nikita – why on earth had she gone looking for *him*?

He wouldn't stop talking – on the doorstep, as he walked in and stood in the sitting room – talking, talking. Robert gestured to a chair and he sat, all the while carrying on in the same soft, *gentle* voice – about his having been out of prison for years, living close by, a family, a wife and children.

At hearing he had been released from prison so long ago Angela looked directly at Robert. He was sure his face showed that he was as surprised to hear all of this as she was, but there was certainly something amounting to reproach in her eyes. But he hadn't known! How could he have known? That was when she'd asked him to go and wait somewhere else. 'Please, Dad, go.' He'd wanted to give a Niki reply – 'It's not my *fault*! It's not *fair*!' Instead he'd said tartly, 'I'll be in the kitchen.'

He supposed he could have found out somehow, but they had put all of that behind them. Why would they have *wanted* to find out? Why dredge up the past – this history where a man had ruined their family life? But now he saw his error. They should have prepared themselves for this possibility – but of course, he had thought Angela and the child gone for good, and Angela in turn had thought the father gone for good. This scenario had just been so outside the realms of possibility.

He absently turned over a page of his newspaper on the kitchen table. They'd been talking for a good five minutes in there – surely they should all be out looking for Niki.

♠♠♠♠

Keeping her finger on the buzzer, Niki waited.

The door opened a couple of inches, restricted by a security chain. Chantelle's face appeared around the edge.

'Niki! Blimey, you're givin' everyone a right scare.' She pushed the door closed again and Niki heard her slide off the chain.

'Is that 'er?' she heard Chantelle's mum calling down the hallway.

'Oh. . .' Niki suddenly felt trapped.

'Yeah, she's 'ere, Mum,' Chantelle shouted back. 'Come in, Nik.'

'You get in 'ere, young lady,' Chantez said, appearing in the sitting room doorway and beckoning them in. She was still in her nurse's uniform and had a brisk, work-like manner about her. Niki had only wanted to see Chantelle and now wished she hadn't come.

'Sit down. Right. I'm gonna call your mum and then I'm takin' you 'ome, clear?'

*'No!'*

'I'm not takin' no messin', d'you get me? We've got a boy lyin' in 'ospital an' you are out there scarin' your poor mother half to death. It's just plain wrong.'

And suddenly Niki was crying.

'Oh, come on, don' *cry*,' said Chantez, her voice a bit softer. 'I'm makin' that call, Niki, 'cause your mum is properly goin' out of 'er 'ead. That's *nice* of 'er, to care like that. It's *nice* to be loved and worried about, so there's no need to go cryin' about it.' Chantez went into the hallway to phone Angela.

'What's goin' on, den, Nik?' Chantelle asked her. They heard Chantez on the phone.

'I'll bring her 'ome soon, Ange. She's just a bit upset, but she's fine, so don' you worry, righ'?' She came back in and sat down, stretching her mouth wide, turning it down at the corners and raising her eyebrows as she waited for Nikita to speak.

'Come on, tell us,' she said when Niki didn't immediately offer an explanation. 'We're listenin'', ain't we, Chan?'

'Yep. Come on, neek,' Chantelle smiled encouragingly and gave Niki a gentle shove.

'How's Tyrone?' Niki asked.

'He's gonna be OK,' Chantelle said. 'He's gonna pull through.'

'Stop stalling,' prompted Chantez.

Niki took a deep breath. 'My mum's found out that

I've been seeing my dad and now she wants us to move back to Oakley and she says it won't stop me seeing him but it *will*, it *will* and I don't *want* to move again and he's not like she thinks he is anyway and she's going to ruin everything! And I *know* I should have done things differently but I didn't have any choice! If my mum had known she'd have said no, so what was the *point*? How *else* could I have seen my dad? It's just not *fair*.'

'OK, back up, Niki. Chantelle, get 'er some water. An' make sure your sisters are still in bed. And tell Shaquille it's time to turn his TV *off*.

'OK. So start again. You found out that your dad lives nearby.'

'Yes. And he's a *good person*. Not like my mum thinks. He has a family – a wife and two little girls. But the wife, *she* doesn't want me being there, I can tell. And so she was saying they've got to tell my mum and—'

'Right, so hold up right there. Your mum didn't know?'

'Well, she does now. She thought my dad was in prison – so did I – but then I found out that he's not, so I went and found him—'

'Without telling your mum.'

'Only 'cause I *knew* she'd not want me to.'

'Isn't that understandable?'

'But he's *different* now. And it was all going really well, but his *wife*—'

'Wanted your mum to know.'

'She says I was there too much and there have to be "boundaries".'

'Well, she sounds pretty sensible if you ask me. Don't look at me like that. They're a family with two little girls – you're seein' them and your *mum* didn't *know*. Of *course* they've got to tell 'er! And – do you know what – her saying that is probably far *more likely* to mean you can keep seein' your dad than if she 'ad gone on encouragin' you to be all secretive, so, actually, she sounds pretty *nice* to me. Pretty understandin', under the circumstances.'

Chantelle had come in and stood next to her mum with a glass of water, which she handed to Niki.

Niki looked down at her hands, too miserable at Chantez's matter-of-fact manner to be able to talk any more. She wanted to be upstairs, just her and Chantelle – not sitting here being told that Dilani sounded like a sensible woman.

'You do realise, Niki, that the only way this'll be sorted out is if you go home? So, I'm gonna walk you there now, OK? Chantelle, you'll have to stay for your sisters and brother.'

'Please don't make me go back. You don't understand. Mum'll make us leave – she always does. Can't I stay here – then she can calm down and then I can talk to her properly.'

Chantez pursed her lips. 'I'm gonna give you the followin' choice: you can either come wiv me right now back to your mum's, or I call the police and say someone is *trespassin'* on my *property*, d'you get me?'

Chantelle gave her a look that said, *she will*!

'So, which is it gonna be?'

# SEVENTEEN

Angela heard Niki's key in the lock and yanked open the door. There was Niki with Chantez.

'Thank you so much,' Angela said.

'She's in a bit of a state, I'm afraid.'

'Thank you.' Angie shepherded Niki through the door.

'Well, I'll leave you to it. If there's anythin' I can do. . .'

'Thanks. Really. We really appreciate it.'

Niki walked into the sitting room. She didn't feel any sense of elation at seeing her dad there. He was sitting in an armchair that appeared too small for him.

Angie came into the room behind her. She didn't touch Niki, didn't envelope her in her arms as she had the last time she'd been missing. Instead, her mum stood, arms by her side, looking strikingly like Grandad.

'So,' said Damien. 'I guess it's best if I go. . . and

perhaps . . . I'll call you?' He looked questioningly at Angela who nodded.

'Bye, Nik. I'm glad you're back safe. Time for a good chat with your mum, yeah? Don't *ever* run away like that again.'

His calling her Nik – shortening her name even further – kissing her on the forehead, telling her what not to do. . . it made Angie want to rush forward and push herself between them.

She followed him into the hall. He held the door open while she thought, will you just go, wanting to slam it right in his face.

'I'm sorry for the shock of it all – for how it's all come to light and that. I know I should have. . .' His voice trailed off.

Angie nodded, chewed her bottom lip, tried to look calm and as though she were taking this all in her stride.

'So. We should talk soon, yeah?'

She nodded her head vigorously, nodding, nodding. Just go, just go.

And finally he was gone. She shut the door quietly, slowly, buying time, because she knew that in a moment she would have to turn and her daughter would go straight for it. That would be Niki. She had kept this little secret but now that it was out, Angela knew that Niki would grip on like Popper, who could hang his whole weight off a ball with his terrier teeth – hanging on for dear life with those little needles so that he would pierce right through and have to prise it off with his paws.

'Happily ever after for him, then, isn't it?' She heard a bitterness in her voice that she hadn't meant to be there. 'A real, live family. Everything you don't have.'

'It's not like that.'

'I'm going to be having words with Hyacinth, that's for sure.'

'She didn't mean to tell me.'

'Well she should have known better.' Angie felt exhausted all of a sudden. 'We used to tell each other everything,' she said. 'When did all these secrets start?'

'I think they started when you lied about Grandma and Grandad,' Niki said.

Angie was still standing at the door, her hand on its latch. She looked at her hand and slowly took it down.

'I thought I was doing what was best for you.'

'Best!'

'I thought they didn't. . .'

'Best? For *me*?'

'I thought they didn't want to know – Dad, anyway.'

'Best for you, more like.'

Angie had seen a whole new side to her father, though – or rather an old side re-emerged. The sort of dad who had winked at her and asked for her help pruning the roses, the sort of grandad who brought his granddaughter a glass of water and as he gave it, laid his hand on her shoulder. The realisation that she had borne her grudge too long only seemed to increase her anger and resentment at him – why hadn't he told her he was sorry, that he'd changed? Why hadn't he waved the white flag and called her home?

'This just isn't working.'

'I didn't mean to hurt you, Mum.'

'It was a mistake to come back.'

'I wasn't going to keep it a secret – just till I knew he was all right, that he wouldn't hurt us.'

'What do you know about him hurting us?' Angela hissed. How could she explain the extent of pain? The hurt wasn't just about being struck across the face while trying to shield a baby in her arms; it wasn't simply seeing the wild eyes of someone so high he couldn't comprehend his own name; or about fighting to stop his taking hold of their child, even with loving intentions, because she knew at the next moment he might scald her or hallucinate her into a monster and throw her across the room.

The hurt was as much about a reformed, fresh-faced, healthy man, with a wife and children, standing on her doorstep. It was as much about a smile that reminded her of all she had never had with him, of all those dreams that had been dashed like a bottle hurled against a wall. That could hurt just as deeply. That could make a person weep.

'I'm sorry,' Niki said.

'You were happy in Oakley.'

Niki shook her head.

'He said you've been visiting too much, you know.'

'Angela,' Robert said appearing in the hallway from the kitchen.

'Oh, you stay out of this.'

'Just be careful, dear, what you say.'

'Don't panic, we'll visit you. No need to worry, *Dad*.'

'Mum,' said Niki.

'And you can still see him,' said Angie, turning back to her. 'When we come and visit Grandad, you can go round. I hear Bea is really going through it trying to care for Peter. *She* needs us. Dad's all right.' She began to head upstairs. It was all so clear what she had to do. It wasn't running away. It was about keeping her daughter safe, protecting her from stabbings, and failing at school, and all these lies.

'Mum!'

'You've only just got here, you can't uproot again!' Robert said, moving to stand next to Niki in the hallway. Angela looked down at their upturned faces. Why was he making this so much harder – he knew the tough decisions parents had to make. Why was he trying to make her doubt herself?

'You hated her being born. Don't pretend!' She ran up the stairs.

Niki pushed past her grandad to follow her mum.

'*Mum!*'

'We're going to pack now and leave tomorrow. A boy in your class has been *stabbed*. Do you hear me? You're cheating on schoolwork. You're lying. . .'

'You can't do this!'

'I can and I will.'

'Be rational, Angela!' Robert had followed as fast as he could; his words came in short gasps.

'Have him take away my daughter? Make her *blame* me for keeping them apart? I didn't *know*—'

'I know, Mum. I'm not trying to make you feel bad.'

'I'm not *saying* you can't see him, OK? I'm just saying – it's all too close with us living here. It can't work like this.'

'Angela,' Robert finally got to just beneath them. He had turned the corner and pulled himself up the few steps that separated the top landing from the bathroom.

Niki pushed past her mum and put one hand against the wall, one hand on the landing banister, barricading Angela's way to the bedrooms.

'*Please!* We're settled here now,' Niki said. 'We move *all* the *time*.'

'This last time wasn't my fault,' Angie said.

'You can't keep running away!' Niki shouted.

Angie stared coldly at her daughter. 'OK. I've had enough of this. Stop shouting at me. Saying something louder doesn't make it mean *more*, you know. I've told you that you can still get to know your father – he's in your life now, so that's it. I'm just saying that *Tooting* isn't working out.'

'It's not *fair*!'

'Get out of my way, Niki.' Angie stepped forwards to get past her, but Niki held up her hands and refused to budge. They gripped each other's hands, interlacing their fingers, like they might suddenly have a game of mercy. 'Niki. Get out of my way.'

'No! I'm not leaving!'

'Come on, girls, calm down.' Robert stepped up and put his hands on Angie's back, trying to soothe her. She was behaving as much like a teenager as her daughter. If only Betsy were here. 'Everyone needs to calm down!'

They tussled, and Angie was surprised to find how strong her daughter was. Somehow she was unbalanced and had to take a step back, pushing into Robert, catching him off guard. He found himself falling, his foot missing the step below, tipping through the open door to the bathroom, arms windmilling, mouth open, eyes wide with surprise; falling back, falling, nothing to stop him, falling, head smacking against the sink.

♦♦♦♦

Angela reacted on autopilot. She could hear herself calling her dad as she knelt down beside him, sliding a hand underneath his head to see whether it came back covered in blood. It took her a moment to register that it hadn't, that her palm was clean, that he was still breathing – she could feel breath through his nostrils gently pushing against her cheek. Everything around her was quiet as though her ears had blocked on the take off of an aeroplane, or from ducking underwater. And from far away she could hear her voice saying, 'Dad? Dad?'

His face was peaceful. His skin hadn't changed colour or temperature. It was as if she had come upstairs and found him asleep on the bathroom floor.

She turned to Niki and talked in a perfectly calm voice, instructing her to phone the ambulance, telling her what to say – 'He's a seventy-seven year old man who's hit his head. He's unconscious, but breathing. Find out how long they'll be, OK? Then phone Hyacinth and get her round. You'll have to stay at hers tonight.'

She turned back to her dad and pulled some towels, warm from the radiator, to lay over him.

'You're going to be OK, Dad, an ambulance is on its way. Dad? Blink if you can hear me. Dad. Squeeze my hand.'

Their proximity to St George's Hospital meant the ambulance was with them in under five minutes. After Niki had made the phone calls and put the door on the latch, she went back upstairs and watched her mother calmly talking to him, never leaving him to lie there in silence. Niki stood by the door rubbing her hand up and down its frame.

Hyacinth arrived at the same time as the paramedics. They seemed enormous coming up the stairs in their green overalls with their boxes of equipment. Her mum stepped back and a woman with mousy hair in a ponytail began talking loudly in a professional sounding voice.

'Mr Smith, hello, Mr Smith, can you hear me? Mr Smith? Can you open your eyes for me? Robert? Open your eyes, Robert.'

Angie spoke to the other paramedic, her voice shaky, her eyes wandering, her arms propelling as she explained how her father had fallen.

'How long has he been unconscious?'

'I don't know, I don't know – seven minutes? Less. He just stepped back but there was no step. He fell straight back – we couldn't do anything.'

'You've hit your head, Robert. That's right. He's conscious, he's talking,' the paramedic said, looking up past Angela to her co-worker.

'Dad!' She could see his lips moving, his eyelids fluttering like little moths trapped under a glass.

'You're all right, Robert, we're going to take you into hospital.'

'It seems like a concussion. He's complaining about his shoulder, too,' the man told Angie. 'I expect we'll keep him in overnight. Check that's all there is to it. He might have dislocated his shoulder, perhaps cracked his wrist. We'll check his skull, but he seems to be made of pretty tough stuff, your dad.'

Robert was carried down the stairs strapped to a chair, his head and neck braced against a board, his arm and wrist protected with padding.

'Dad,' Angie said as he came down to where she stood at the bottom of the stairs. 'Where's your medication? I need to give them your medication so they know what you take.'

'No, no,' he whispered. He had turned paler and he seemed to have trouble focusing on her.

Niki stood in the sitting room watching him be manoeuvred slowly out of the front door. Hyacinth sat in an armchair saying, 'Oh deardeardear, mymymy.' He looked frailer than Niki had ever seen him, strapped into that chair, small and bony. She had a sudden, stark picture of what he'd look like dead.

'Dad, your medication,' said Angie, still following.

'No,' he said.

'It's OK to give it to them, they're helping you. It's important.' She trailed behind the woman paramedic as they stepped outside. The flashing lights of the ambulance pulsed into the night sky. Across the road Angela could see people watching through their curtains. Some had even stepped outside.

'I don't know where he keeps it all, it must be in his room. It's all in a plastic box divided up for the days of the week. He's got cancer, he won't tell me much – I think primary. Recently diagnosed. . . he won't tell me.

'Dad, we need to know. It'll make things much easier for them at the hospital.'

They transferred him onto a trolley-bed – as though he were as light as a child – and manoeuvred it into the ambulance.

'Vitamins.'

'He's saying something,' said the male paramedic who was now in the ambulance next to him. He held out a hand and helped Angie step up next to him. She leant her ear close to her father.

'Come on, Dad. We're not going to leave you, OK? You can tell me.'

'Vitamins. They're just vitamins. I made the whole thing up.'

She stood up straight and looked down at him, then at the paramedic.

'I'll get his things and follow you,' she said.

'So?' said the woman paramedic outside.

'No. I'm mistaken – he's not currently on anything. He must. . . be. . . in remission.' She felt a giggle surging up inside her like an air bubble and ran off towards the house.

Inside, Hyacinth said, 'You don' worry 'bout Niki, she come wid me. Stay de night, nah. You go on, Angie. He gonna be fine – man like Rabert is like a *rock*. Nuttin' gonna break 'im.'

'Thank you, Hyacinth.' She looked at Niki whose face was heart-achingly forlorn. How could she have shouted at her – said such awful things?

'Love.' She pulled her into a hug and rejoiced at the fierceness of Niki's hug back. 'You be good. It's your first day back at school tomorrow. I think you should sleep at Hyacinth's because I don't know what time I'll be back. Hyacinth, she hasn't had any dinner either. Love, I'll call and let you know the update, but Grandad is going to be *fine,* OK? You should try to go to school if you can – it'll keep your mind off things. Try to get some sleep and *don't worry.*' She held Niki's face in her hands and kissed her on the cheek.

'Leave 'er to me. She in good 'ands.'

'Thank you, Hyacinth,' Angela said, realising then that she wouldn't be having any 'words' with this sweet woman, who had at many times been like a second mother to her.

'Do I *have* to go to school?'

'You should go, darling.'

She wanted to tell Niki that she thought Grandad was going to be finer, in fact, than she could have imagined, but first she wanted to be absolutely sure. Vitamins!

Niki's lips started wobbling. 'I didn't mean to. . .'

'Honey. We all behaved *ridiculously* tonight. Well, I did. If it was anyone's fault, it was mine. It was an accident. Life's too short for casting blame and bearing grudges.' She felt herself releasing grudges and blame like birds thrown into the air from outstretched hands. Life was too short for looking backwards.

'Try to sleep well.' She hugged Niki and kissed her again, then ran inside to pack an overnight bag for her dad.

Niki stood outside with Hyacinth, who patted her arm.

'Don' you worry. 'E's 'ad a poorly turn, 'e'll be fine.'

'He fell.'

'Poor man. Dear dear. 'E in good 'ands, darlin'. Don' you worry. You come eat some dinner. Don' you worry 'bout 'im. You come wid me and we eat our dinner, den we get your jammies after dat, OK? Come on, chil'.'

♠♠♠♠

As Angie packed – feverishly, smiling and shaking as though she'd drunk too much caffeine – she realised how much she wasn't ready to let him go. How sorry she was for everything, all that time of turning her back on him, all her cold punishing of him ever since they'd returned, refusing to let him forget his shortcomings. She realised that she *didn't* hold a catalogue of criticisms against him any more. They had vanished in a moment, like smoke cupped in her hands. And it was wonderful, that relief. She tried to hurry, her hands fumbling to stuff his slippers, a book, a clean set of clothes into his bag so that she could get to him as quickly as possible to reassure him of her change of heart.

She laughed as she opened the top drawer of her dad's bedside table. Why hadn't she pushed him further about his illness? She chided herself with a smile. Those fake doctor's appointments. The way he'd alluded to so much but never actually said anything concrete. She'd just taken it as a given – thought him surprisingly healthy but, well, there had been all those pills he'd lined up each morning next to his toast and tea, popping them into his mouth one by one. Struggling to swallow them down his gullet, gulping so that his Adam's apple slid up and down his slack-skinned throat, making her think of a tortoise. She looked in the drawer at packets of vitamin C, D, A-Z Gold, aspirin, laxatives. She loved him for his ridiculous charade. A bump to the head. Perhaps an injured shoulder or arm. Seventy-seven and essentially as fit as a fiddle.

This little deception now exposed, it was the most expressive thing he'd done in her memory – the white flag *had* been waved.

By his bed was a photo of Betsy holding baby Angela in her arms in a frame. And next to that a curling photo of Nikita that Angela remembered sending to Betsy long ago.

Her own irrational solutions for dealing with the shock of Niki unearthing Damien made her see her father's methods of coping in a new light. She could see him so much more clearly now, could understand why her mum had continued to defend him and tell her that he would eventually come round. She realised he'd probably wanted to come round for years but that she had made it impossible for him.

'Oh, Dad,' she said with a smile and headed out of the front door, jogging all the way to the hospital, too impatient to walk.

◆◆◆◆

Robert hadn't finished being examined. A nurse had been with him and he'd been X-rayed, and now he was waiting for a doctor before he would be allocated a bed. He lay on a trolley, staring at the white ceiling tiles and listening to constant movement going on beyond his curtained cubicle.

'Hi, Dad,' Angie said and sat down beside him.

'Angela.' He held out his unhurt hand and she took hold of it.

'We've had quite the night, eh?'

He smiled. He still looked pale and his grip was weak. She squeezed his hand, thinking of how he might have been taken from her. She might have realised too late that she forgave him. Withholding forgiveness, bearing grudges, it was all pointless.

Everyone hurt everyone. Everyone let everyone down. It was human nature, human frailty. Giving each other a break was, she decided, the only option.

'I'm sorry, Dad. I don't know what came over me.'

'You never told us what really happened – never told your mother, even. Not everything. I thought you'd have talked with your mother.'

'Water under the bridge.'

'We shouldn't bottle things up though, love, that's fatal. That leads to corrosion inside – that makes things remain with us much longer. We need to let it all out.'

'Let it all out?' she said with a smile.

'I was alive in the sixties, you know,' he said with a weak smile back. He extracted his hand from Angela's grasp and lightly pressed his head, closing his eyes as he did so. He had a throbbing headache and felt very tired.

'Is it so bad,' he asked after a moment, opening his eyes again, 'that Nikita wants to see her father?'

'I don't know. It appears he's "changed".'

'Are you convinced?'

'Well, a lot of time has passed. He certainly looks different.' He had looked, Angie thought, like when she'd first met him. In the early days before the drugs had infected his mind with desperation and paranoia.

'I don't know. I guess I'll have to meet him again for a proper talk – see if he's for real. I just couldn't bear him hurting Niki – she's attached to him already. I had no idea she longed for him so much.'

'She probably didn't realise it herself,' Robert said. 'But to find out someone you thought was in prison was living so close, and seemingly a very different person from all you'd presumed. . . surely you wouldn't have passed up such an opportunity if you'd been in her shoes?'

'I suppose not.'

♦♦♦♦

'So – in the ambulance – you talked about staying. . .' he said, just before he was taken away.

'Oh, you heard *that* bit did you?' Angie said, smiling. 'Well, it looks that way. . . I should have guessed, you know. When I first saw you, I didn't think you looked ill.'

# EIGHTEEN

Nikita played with the food on her plate. Chilli tingled on her lips and left her tongue burning long after she'd swallowed her meagre forkful.

'Not 'ungry?'

'Not really. I might just go to bed.' The tears were welling up again. How could they leave Grandad now that she'd almost killed him? What if his head had been cracked right open? What if they hadn't been there – if he'd just slipped and fallen while on his own? Who would have helped him then? But it was she who had forced her mother's hand. She knew how it worked: her mum had now said one thing – that they were going – so that meant she couldn't back down. They were tied in and there was nothing that could be done.

What had her dad *done* to her mum? Why was she so unable to talk about him? Why the need to run away?

To have found that all her worst nightmares were merely that, make-believe lies that could never hurt her again. And now it was all being pulled away from her, as if she was clutching a jumper tighter and tighter while someone pulled a thread so that all she could do was watch it unravel in her hands.

'Go into de sittin' room. We watch telly and I get you some puddin'.'

Niki flicked through the channels – documentaries and the news seemed to be the only things on.

'I guess de news is de only one wort' watchin' of de options?' Hyacinth handed her a bowl of vanilla ice cream and a soup spoon.

'Thank you.'

Going back to St Magda's. It wasn't the worst thing that could happen, she realised. Going back to Mrs M and Peter, to Popper. These were all wonderful things. If someone had asked her, even up to a few weeks ago, she would probably have said yes to it all.

But now. She didn't have another friend like Chantelle. And as much as she loved the Munroes, her loyalty was to Grandad. And there was Hyacinth to think about... It wasn't just about Damien, she wanted to say to her mum. Now she would pick Tooting over Oakley, because it felt like home. She fitted.

♦♦♦♦

'Water under the bridge,' Angela had said.

Yes, thought Robert, as he lay awake on the ward, Angie sleeping in a chair next to him. His head seemed to be throbbing more. He closed his eyes and saw swirling colours of greens and yellows and reds. His eyes felt hot.

On his way to the hospital, thoughts had swum before him as he slipped in and out of consciousness – his wife's laughing face on the first day he'd met her; her holding their precious daughter on Angela's first birthday, blowing out the candle over Angie's shoulder, clapping Angie's hands together. And then those moments when Angela had rushed to hug him as a child.

Maybe one day he would tell his daughter. But what purpose would it serve? He didn't want to keep bottling it up, but why dredge up what's been laid to rest? Move on. Clean break. That was the answer.

Catherine, her name had been – big hipped, wore terrible cardigans and flowery skirts with elasticated waists. It had been one of those ridiculous moments, like something from a soap opera. Working late. Everyone gone. She taught music, was writing reports in the staff room. He had finished his after-school chess club. He'd come in to gather his marking.

Betsy was at home, pregnant. So, he had betrayed them both – Betsy *and* Angela. He had been so fixated on the thought that the baby surely couldn't be his – and somehow this seemed to justify what happened.

She wasn't even his type, but he could see that she liked him. In that flustery, spinsterish way of someone who hadn't been touched by a man in who-knew-how-long. Her bosom had heaved and her coffee-scented breath panted so deeply, luxuriously – *musically* – that he had realised she wasn't devoid of a certain amount of experience. It had been awful from first to last.

It made his skin crawl to think of it even now. It had made him struggle to have sex with Betsy after, because every time he looked down at her trusting face, her open arms, all he could think of was that other, flushed face, and those clammy, enfolding arms that had been as cloying as her overpowering perfume.

The act, on a staffroom settee of all places. What had *possessed* him? He had turned and she had been right behind him. His hand had brushed against her bosom and he had blushed. She had given a coquettish sort of laugh. He couldn't remember how it was that he was suddenly kissing her wide, lipsticked mouth. There had been too much saliva, too much suction. Her thighs were bigger than he was used to – he had felt consumed.

It had all been so humiliating. Trousers round his ankles, her hideous skirt up about her waist, on her back like some sort of capsized beetle. The images had come back again and again throughout his married life, provoking a self-loathing that would cause him to grind his nails into his hand, pinch and twist at his skin. It wasn't anything personal against *her*, against Catherine, the level of his distaste. But just that he had done these things with anyone other than his wife.

He had watched Betsy swell gently – ripening, with such a glow about her – completely unsuspecting, not understanding why it was that he became colder and colder.

And then Angela was born. She was born and she grew. And with every passing year he saw that there was no mistaking her. She was *his* child, all right, his daughter, an absolute chip: the same marble-white skin, the same November eyes. She didn't even have her mother's dark hair but his fair wispiness instead. It was like a fresh accusation every time she smiled at him with his smile, or looked at him with his eyes.

He would never want Angela to know this. And he was sure – it wasn't deception, he really was sure – that Betsy would not want him to tell her either. But he called to Betsy, I'm sorry, I'm so, so sorry – a final purging. He could feel the freedom, letting his burden go like a helium balloon, up, up, up and then, at last, gone.

He saw finally that in punishing himself he had only served to punish those he cared for most. There was only so long a person could look back and carry a ball and chain of past mistakes. But now, Angela and Nikita had returned to him and this was his chance – his final chance – to make amends. And he would do that not by wallowing in his guilt, but by letting it go.

And another thing he'd do, he thought with a smile – feeling sleep finally drawing him, and with a sense of Betsy by his bedside – was buy some new pyjamas.

♦♦♦♦

The next morning, Niki went home to shower and get ready for school. Hyacinth came with her, made her sit and eat a proper breakfast, and then waved her off from the front door.

Chantelle had been allowed to see Tyrone the day before. Niki, Chantelle and Sangeeta spent their lunch break in the Art Room, making him a comic. While they drew, Niki filled them in on all that had happened, telling Sangeeta about her father, telling them both about her grandad hitting his head.

'We're moving back to Oakley.'

'That sucks.'

'I'm sorry, Niki,' said Sangeeta.

'You'd better stay in touch, mind, Neekster.'

♦♦♦♦

Outside the school gates at the end of the day, Niki heard someone calling her name. She saw Damien sitting in his car.

'That's my dad,' Niki said.

The three girls walked over.

'Hi, Niki. I wondered if I could have a chat with you?'

'Will your mum mind?' Sangeeta asked.

'She knows,' said Damien. 'She's said it's OK.'

Chantelle and Sangeeta walked off together, glancing back over their shoulders while Niki waited for Damien to lock his car and put his coat on.

'I can walk you home.'

'OK.'

It struck Niki that they wouldn't seem an unusual sight to passers-by. People would just see a father and daughter walking side by side, as though they'd been doing it all their lives.

'You've imagined all kinds of things about me while you've been growing up, I expect. . . And some of what I want to tell you, you might not want to hear.'

Niki felt a knot tightening in her stomach. All the horror stories that she had conjured up over the years had been erased in just a few weeks of seeing her dad smile, seeing him love his daughters, seeing him welcome her like – well, like a long-lost daughter. She didn't want this new 'everything's forgiven' image replaced with concrete facts that might confirm the shadowy nightmares that had lurked inside her for too long.

'In many ways I don't want to,' said Damien. 'But you need to know what I was like. You need to know who I am. And I think it'll help you understand where your mum is coming from a bit more. Nik?'

He stopped and looked at her. She could feel his eyes on her as she kept looking at her feet.

'One of the things about my getting off drugs and

living in the real world is having to be honest. Living with lies is really destructive. So can I go on?'

Still looking at her shoes, she nodded.

He guided her with his hand to get them walking again. It was easier to hear him talk without having to look at him, so she was glad they were side by side rather than facing each other.

'The truth is, I was an awful person. I *did* hit your mother. That was one of the first questions you ever asked me and I didn't answer you then. So that's my answer. Yes, I hit your mother.

'It's not that I didn't care for her when we first met – but we were far too young. And when you came along, I just wasn't ready for that kind of responsibility. I stood by her, but grudgingly. I made it impossible for her – I never let her forget that she was this unwanted burden.

'We were kind of OK to begin with. But when she moved in – well, you were quite a difficult baby. We didn't have a clue what we were doing. And I was starting to go off the rails. Really, from as soon as I found out she was pregnant I went into a bit of a spiral. It was panic, I guess.'

Niki's chest and throat felt tight. She didn't know if he was expecting her to respond when he paused, but she kept quiet, unable to think of anything to say.

'Please understand. I'm not saying any of this is your fault. I'm not saying that I wish you weren't here, OK? You're my daughter and I would never want to be without you.' He put his hand on her shoulder, and Niki felt compelled to glance up at him. She nodded and tried to smile as if she believed him.

'She was a young girl trying to be a mum, Angie was. And I was a mess. She had to *hide* you from me. I hate myself for what I put you two through – and saying, "oh, it was the drugs" doesn't excuse it. I treated her like this utter piece of . . . well, as really unwelcome in *my* house, in *my* life.

'It wasn't like I was always doing horrible things to *you*. It was more that I didn't know *what* I was doing, so she couldn't trust me. She'd hear me come in and have to guess what sort of mood I was in. She sometimes had to lock the two of you in the bathroom with me hammering on the door. She hid you in the loft, under the bed . . . sometimes you would cry and give the game away.

'I wasn't trying to find you to hurt you – I did love you. I wanted to see you to show you off to mates, or just for a cuddle, but if you started crying then I didn't know how to shut you up, and then your mum'd be scared because I might start shaking you or shouting at you. Which, of course, made you bawl even more. So, as time went on you would cry whenever I came near you, because you were frightened.' He rubbed his face roughly with both hands.

'Once, I took you without her knowing and drove with you on the passenger seat of the car – just lying there, nothing holding you in, rolling round like a doll – totally off my head. I did that.'

She could hear his voice cracking.

'I could have killed you. Niki. I did terrible, terrible things. I promise you I am here for you now and I will do my best to be the dad I should have been.'

He stopped talking.

Niki thought, I just need to keep my eyes down, keep looking at this pavement, keep walking – because otherwise everything will start spinning and I won't be able to stand. She could feel him looking at her, waiting, his hands pushed deep into the pockets of his jacket.

'There's a lot to get your head round. I am saved from drugs, from all the rubbish that I got myself messed up with, but that doesn't change what I did. I almost destroyed my entire family – my parents, my brothers and sister. . . I understand that you might not want to see me after hearing this.'

She thought about her dad driving along with a tiny baby rolling about on the car seat next to him. She supposed that the sick feeling that had exploded inside her as she watched her grandfather's skull smack against the curved edge of the sink must have been something like the sensation of finding your baby gone and knowing she was with someone who was probably off his face.

She imagined her mum, a teenager, sliding a baby under a bed; cowering in a bathroom while Damien hammered his fists on the door; shutting the door to the attic and praying her baby wouldn't start screaming and give away her hiding place.

It was hard to resolve these ideas with the Damien she had been getting to know, thought she knew. She'd been so certain that she was right and her mum was wrong.

♦♦♦♦

How on earth would she tell Niki, wondered Angie, sitting with her head in her hands. She had returned to the hospital after lunch to be ushered into a room and asked to sit down.

'What's wrong, what is it? He doesn't have cancer, he made it up.'

'I'm very sorry, Miss Smith.'

Angie felt the tears coming before the nurse went any further.

This can't be happening, she thought, hardly able to take in all that was being said.

'He went very peacefully.'

'But he was fine! I left him only a few hours ago and all he had was a headache. They X-rayed him and everything.'

'He suffered from shock, and there was a bleed that wasn't apparent at first. He deteriorated very quickly.'

'But he seemed so *well*, so himself. . .'

He'd been lovely, she thought. The way they'd talked, and his smile that had accepted her, understood, and made their whole relationship new. And now there was no time to enjoy it. He'd gone.

♠♠♠♠

Angie sat on the edge of Niki's bed and stroked her hair.

'So, are you doing OK?' she asked.

'I don't know.' Niki had done a lot of crying since

arriving back home to find Angela waiting with a blank look of shock.

She'd cried for her grandfather, for all her dad had told her, for all that her mum had been through. The corners of her eyes stung and she felt exhausted.

'You know, I misjudged your grandad a lot,' Angie said, twisting Niki's hair slowly between her fingers. 'He loved you very much. All along.'

'And you.'

'Yes,' Angie gave a small smile and found the tears coming again.

'What'll happen now?'

'What do you mean? The funeral? I don't know, we'll think about it tomorrow.'

It felt strange to be dealing with all these things at once. Niki couldn't believe her grandad was really gone, just like that. She kept expecting to hear his feet coming slowly up the stairs, his trembling voice calling out with offers of tea.

And then there was her time with Damien that afternoon. 'Dad told me stuff,' she said eventually.

'You don't need to worry about that.'

'I'm sorry.'

'Love, let's just leave it behind, hey? I'm not saying we're all going to be eating Christmas dinner together, but you at least can go on seeing him. We've agreed to meet and chat about it – work out how often you go round there and such like. We'll just have to see how it goes.'

Niki twisted the edge of her duvet in her fist. 'What about you?' she asked.

'I've no idea, love, my head is spinning. I can't believe he's gone.' She cried again and Niki reached out for her hand.

'I told Grandad we'd be staying,' continued Angie wiping her eyes on her sleeve. 'And I guess we will. I've got to stop moving at some point, haven't I? You were right about that. . . I'll have to get a job, I guess. . . Oh, I can't think about it now,' she said, her lip trembling.

Niki turned onto her side and shut her eyes. She felt desperately sorry for her mum – sorry and protective from all that she now knew. She thought about the gymnast leaping in the photograph under her bed and decided that she would have to pull it out sometime, in a week or so, and show her mother what she looked like, because, Niki realised, along the way her mum had forgotten.

She couldn't decide whether she felt older or younger than before. Older in starting to love her grandad, only to have him taken away without a goodbye.

Older in having the world open up in complicated, multi-layered ways. Didn't it take an adult's eye to recognise that no one was perfect? Everyone had secrets. Everyone had fears, frailty, longings.

And yet, to see it caused her to feel a twisting disquiet inside her, cold and slender; a sliver of knowledge that would always be with her now. She realised that all those layers inside people meant she couldn't truly know anyone, not absolutely; couldn't just presume, just trust. She had to accept that human weakness meant the people she relied on would let her down. *Would*. Not might.

And this future expectation of hurt, of people dying, people being weak – it had to be something that was OK simply because there was no way round it. It had to be accepted because there was no choice.

And this year she would turn fifteen.

But for now, she was just glad to have her mum sitting on her bed, stroking her hair.

♦♦♦♦

'Oh my days! 'E's so cuuute!'

'Yeah.' Niki smoothed her new puppy's silky body to her cheek, laughing as his blunt little face kept stretching round to lick her chin.

''E's so small, you could fit 'im in yer bag!'

'He's gonna be way tougher than a handbag dog, thank you very much. Ugh! I'm not that sad.'

'Ooh, sorry for breathin'. . . Look at you, tellin' me what's cool!'

'D'you wanna hold him?' Niki handed him over. Sangeeta, sitting next to Chantelle, leant in to give him a tentative stroke, jerking away when he started snuffling at her hand.

'They're a bit dirty, aren't they, animals?' she said. 'I mean, having animals in your house.'

'Awww! 'Ow can you say dat?' Chantelle said, pushing him towards Sangeeta and speaking in a puppy voice, 'Say, "I'm a gorgeous doggy-woggy. Say ya love me."'

'Get away! I admit he's very sweet. But my hands now smell of dog.'

'Thanks for coming today,' Niki said to them both, hugging her knees.

'No worries,' Chantelle replied, handing the puppy back to Niki. 'It were, y'know, sad but good, weren' it?'

'Yes,' Niki agreed. 'Sad but good.'

The funeral had been small, Robert being a private person. 'Intimate,' as Angie had described it. Afterwards, Hyacinth, Chantelle and Chantez, Sangeeta, and Beatrice, who'd arrived to stay for a few days, had come back to the house for tea and Battenberg.

Chantez, Hyacinth and Beatrice were still downstairs with Angie, while the girls were now sitting on Niki's bedroom floor, leaning their backs against her bed.

During the tea, Beatrice had nipped into the back garden and then returned with Popper, holding a cardboard box under one arm. Popper had peed all over the floor in his excitement at seeing Niki.

'You'll have to get used to things like that for a while,' said Beatrice, pushing the box towards Niki.

Niki stared at her mum, grinning, not daring to believe it.

Angie smiled back. 'Open it up, then.'

And there he was inside – a mini-Popper.

'It turns out your old friend has a rather long-standing relationship with one of our neighbour's Jacks,' Beatrice said. 'So you have a certified pedigree there, and one of Popper's very own offspring. I mentioned them in passing to your mum on the phone the other day, and that set her thinking.'

'Seriously?' Niki asked.

Angie nodded. 'Walks every day, mind, and he's not sleeping in your bed.'

'So, what you gonna call 'im?' Chantelle cooed. 'I still can't believe you're allowed a dog – my mum'd never go for dat!'

When sorting through some of Robert's papers, Niki and Angela had found letters sent between Robert and Betsy before they were married. *To my darling Bobsy-Boy. . . From your ever-loving Betsy.*

Niki looked at her friends. She thought of Chantez downstairs – a new friend for her mum, who'd bonded with her over the complexities of teenage daughters.

Even without Damien, Dilani and the girls here, Niki realised that her family had grown – just as she'd longed it would.

And, in a funny way, it was all thanks to her grandad calling them home.

'I'm gonna call him Bobsy,' she said.

## Acknowledgements

My thanks to my agent, Lucy Juckes, for your sharp eye, wisdom and unwavering confidence.

Thank you, too, to Mary Davis for being such an essential link – and your support and example that go so far beyond this book.

To Nkem Okorie, Lisa James and Emily Juckes, my invaluable teen readers, for giving me such useful feedback, and some choice vocab!

Thank you to Meg Wang and Jodie Gaudet: always my first readers and dear friends – I look forward to seeing my name similarly mentioned before too long!

To the whole team at Frances Lincoln for your fantastic efforts in looking after every detail with such commitment – especially Emily Sharratt and Maurice Lyon. You are a pleasure to work with.

To my parents, Philip and Bridget, and wider family, who've supported me along the way. Thank you for always thinking my writing is brilliant and never telling me to be more realistic in my ambitions!

And to my husband, Andy. . . Thank You.

**Zannah Kearns**

is a first-time author who grew up in a village near St Albans. She studied English Literature at Cardiff University, and later returned there to complete an MA in Creative Writing. She has spent most of her professional life working with teenagers – from Costa Rica to UK inner cities. She has also worked in Communications in the charity sector. Zannah lives in Maidenhead with her husband and two young children.

Visit Zannah's website at www.zannahkearns.com and follow her on Twitter @zannahkearns.